Stylite: Romance

Book Three in The Stylite Chronicles

Tag Gregory
Lily Marie

Contents

The Stylite Chronicles

~*~

A Mystery, History, Romance

~*~

*****

Book Three

Stylite: Liberty

*****

Chapter 1

Shower

"Ta da!" I burbled happily, holding up the notebook I'd liberated from the basement of the Hotel Liberty as soon as I reached Brandon.

"That's it? You've been gone, like, an hour, and all you found was one moldy old pocket-sized notebook? Seriously?" Brandon grumbled.

"I wasn't gone an hour, you big worrywort," I corrected him with a chuckle. "It was more like ten minutes, tops. I barely had enough time to look around before you were ordering me to come back."

"Felt like an hour to me," Eggy mumbled under his breath.

"Well, however long it was, I managed to use my time well," I answered politically so as not to cause a fight. "You won't believe what I found over there. It's so cool. I only brought back this one book because most of the other stuff was too bulky to carry - plus I really didn't go over there to steal stuff…"

Brandon snorted, which I chose to ignore as I continued on with my story.

". . . but I don't think anyone will miss this one little book. Besides, I wasn't going to pass up the chance to read what's in here!"

I was waving the small, dusty, leather-bound notebook in Brandon's face as I spoke. This turned out to be too much for my OCD boyfriend, who promptly stepped backwards, far enough away that I couldn't touch him with the potentially contaminated object. Apparently, compulsions top curiosity in this instance.

"What's so special about it?" he asked once he'd retreated to a safe distance.

"This little book happens to be the journal of our dear, sweet, young Billy Carnegie . . ."

"No shit?" Brandon finally seemed impressed by my find.

"And that's not all I found. Wait till you see the pictures I took! Come on, let's head upstairs and I'll show you everything."

"Okay. But . . ."

"But what?" I asked, wondering why he was looking at me with his nose all scrunched up like that.

"Maybe you might like to take a shower first?" Eggy suggested. "You look like one of those chimney sweeps from Mary Poppins."

I looked down at myself and noticed for the first time just how much dirt and dust was coating my clothing after my foray into the bowels of the Hotel Liberty. No wonder Egbert was squicked just looking at me. I must have carted at least half the filth from that basement room back out with me. Looking at all the dirt on my clothing made me realize that was likely the reason my breathing had been getting a little ragged. Damn asthma. Brandon was probably right that a nice long shower should be next on the agenda.

We quickly secured the tunnel door with its chest of drawers blockade and made our way out of the secret room and through the basement. I found my trusty messenger bag where I'd left it on the floor by the basement door and fished through it till I found my inhaler, taking a nice long hit of Albuterol. Then, as soon as my airways felt less constricted, we climbed the stairs back to Eggy's rooms and he pointed me towards the bathroom forthwith. I was happy to go, but not alone.

"You gonna join me, Big Guy?" I asked coyly, tilting my head towards the bathroom door with what I hoped was an inviting smile on my lips.

"I think you're capable of taking a shower all by yourself without falling over this time," he waffled.

"Of course I CAN shower by myself, but where's the fun in that?" I replied saucily. "Besides, I might have some dirty spots I can't reach by myself and you wouldn't want that, now would you?" He was smiling now and looking at me with more than just a little interest. "Come on. I'll let you wash my back and get me super-squeaky clean all over . . ."

"There you go with those ulterior motives again," he protested.

He didn't resist, though, when I reached out, snagged the hem of the shirt he was wearing, and doggedly towed him after me into the bathroom. I must really be good at this hermit therapy thing, you know, because a month before he wouldn't have let me touch him even that much. Thankfully, he was much more compliant these days. So, when I had him where I wanted him - complacently standing in the middle of the bathroom - I took it one step further and reached up to begin unbuttoning his shirt. He didn't even flinch.

I took my time going button to button and then sliding the fabric off Brandon's shoulders, enjoying for a moment the fact that I was being granted so much unfettered access to touch him.

Once I had him bare from the waist up, I allowed my fingers to trail over his smooth chest. I marvelled at the golden tan of his skin, despite the fact that he rarely, if ever, got out in the sun, figuring it must be his natural skin tone. My paler hand resting against his pec showed off the difference amazingly, and for an instant I almost forgot what I was supposed to be doing other than just running my hands over his beautiful skin.

"You next," Brandon directed, fingering the hem of my shirt, still seemingly too nervous about my dirty clothing to fully enjoy my fondling.

"I'm getting there," I advised with a chuckle as I pulled the filthy thing off over my head, raising a small cloud of dust in the process.

Brandon stepped away from me and pointed nervously to the laundry hamper. While I was there I slid off my pants as well, tossing it all in together and leaving me wearing nothing but my birthday suit. As I turned around, I caught my Eggy getting a nice eyeful of my tushie, which made me blush for some reason. It's not like I cared about being naked around him, but there was something about the fact that he was obviously appreciative of my assets that left me flushed and strangely disconcerted. Brandon was such a contradiction in every way; how he managed to be so sensual and at the same time untouchable, was a mystery. One that I was almost as eager to solve as the mystery of his building.

As soon as I was freed of the worst of my dirtiness, he let me approach again and I was allowed to resume my touching of his glorious skin. This time I remained conscious of my goal, though, and guided my trailing fingers lower and lower till I came into contact with the waistband of the jeans he was wearing. It took no time at all to undo the top button and then unzip the fly all the way. Meanwhile, my man stood there and let me undress him like a Ken doll, not helping but not stopping me and, shit, if that didn't make it even hotter. I felt like he was giving himself up to me and allowing me all the control which, for him, was really something. He didn't even bat an eye when I slid my hands inside the back of the now loose jeans and cupped a firm butt cheek in each palm as I pushed the pants below his hips.

"Mmmm," his barely vocal purr sounded loud in the enclosed space of the bathroom as I spent a minute or two kneading at the globes of flesh.

"You know, for a big guy, you have a remarkably compact ass," I commented, getting a scowl from the object of my observation. "I mean that in a good way!" I rushed to correct his assumption. "It's just that you fit so perfectly in my hands. It's like your ass was made for me to fondle."

"Did I mention how weird you are?" was his only response.

"Maybe once or twice," I teased.

Meanwhile, I noted that he hadn't yet pulled away from me or taken any other action to halt my explorations of his nether regions, something that I was rather impressed by, to be honest. I shuffled a few inches closer, allowing my hardening dick to brush against his, all the time prepared for him to reach the limits of his comfort zone and tell me to stop. But he didn't. So I followed up by leaning forward and depositing a line of kisses up the column of his neck, beginning on his bare collarbone and proceeding upward at an angle.

When I eventually reached his ear, I gave the lobe a friendly little nibble and whispered, "at this rate I'm never gonna get that shower."

My teasing seemed to break the tension of the moment and we both laughed. Brandon moved away first, pulling open the door to the shower enclosure and reaching in to start the water running. I waited as patiently as I could, considering the state of lust I was in after that energizing make out session. When all was ready, he stepped in, under the water, and I followed. He handed me the bar of soap and just when I was about to rub it all over my body, I quickly changed my mind. I rubbed the soap between my hands, making sure I got a decent amount of foam to work with. I could feel Brandon watching as I rubbed over my slippery chest, down my abs and over my package, making sure I was nice and lathered. Then I handed the soap over to him and smiled as he did the same. His hands mirroring mine perfectly.

Damn, how I wanted it to be MY hands that were caressing that beautiful body!

But we hadn't done that yet and I didn't know how far my Eggy was willing to let me go. It was killing me, though, not to touch him right then. He was so statuesque, standing there like a fucking adonis, with water dripping off all his parts and the bubbles from the soap dripping down his pecs, flowing into the well of his navel, and then overflowing to trickle down through his pubes like some licentious Galton Board, until all the drips coalesced together into one stream that drizzled off the tip of his hardening cock. When his hand drifted down to wash his ball sac I think I moaned aloud.

"You're drooling," Brandon commented, rightly, with a smirk at my piteousness.

"Can you blame me?" I gestured to the image he was creating and sighed. "To have all THAT right in front of me and not be able to do anything about it? It's just fucking cruel, is what it is, Egbert."

"Who said you couldn't do anything about it?" he asked with a flirtatious little smile that immediately hit some chord deep inside me.

"Halle-fucking-lujah!" I mumbled and immediately took him up on his invitation, stepping forward, capturing the hand that was currently playing with his soapy balls and taking over the washing duties with a happy moan.

I started with a bit of general fondling, just letting my hand cup underneath the swelling of his small but firm balls and then gliding upwards, circling around the fullness of his penis as it hardened at my touch, ending with a happy little tug. Brandon mmmm'd at me, his eyes closed and a half-smile on his lips. Since he was obviously enjoying himself, and not freaking out over all the touching, I felt emboldened. I took a better hold on the object of my focus, enjoying the heft of his dick lying against my palm, filling and plumping with each beat of his heart. I let the soap act as a lubricant as I slowly and deliberately slid my fingers up and down the silky smooth shaft, pulling him towards me a little bit with each motion, until there was barely an inch between us. Then, with my free hand, I reached out, grabbed his wrist, and guided his hand to my own straining cock. He hesitated only an instant before he grabbed hold, his grip was firmer than I had expected, which pleased me immensely.

Then we just went for it like fiends!

So, yeah, mutual hand jobs may sound a bit juvenile to some of you. I get it that you probably think I'm being a little overboard in my enthusiasm here. But I'm not sure if you understand just how monumental this development was for my OCD Hermit Boy. Cuz, guys, there's nothing quite so messy as dueling hand jobs - assuming you do it right - with cum flying everywhere and so much touching of genitals and just the general unsanitariness of it all . . . The fact we were in the shower obviously helped a lot, because all the water and soap probably countered Brandon's anxiety to a large extent. But still, can I just say, HOT, FUCKING, DAMN!

Needless to say, neither one of us lasted all that long. A few dozen strokes and we were both cumming buckets. I loved the little jerk and twitch of his cock in my hand as he shot, followed by the groan of repletion as his body sagged against my own. I followed suit half a second later, my head cushioned against his strong pec and one arm wrapped tightly around his waist, holding us together and upright. Then we just clung to each other for fuck knew how many minutes, inhaling the sandalwood aroma of his soap while the warm water showered down over our bodies, rinsing away all evidence of our lust and refreshing us at the same time.

As if that wasn't miraculous enough, however, our shower ended with yet another milestone. When we'd both finally caught our breath, Brandon leaned over, used one long index finger positioned under my chin to tilt my face upward, and initiated a kiss for the very first time! I was so surprised I almost forgot to kiss back at first.

"I think we're both clean enough by this point," Brandon announced when he finally pulled away, reaching out to shut off the water.

I was still too caught up in that amazing kiss to say anything and simply tripped along after him in a happy daze.

All fresh and clean from our shower, I followed Brandon into his room where he handed over a clean pair of sweats for me to put on since my clothing was now quarantined in his laundry hamper. I guess I was still a little tired from my marathon Diner shifts the past few days because that, plus the happy lassitude after our shower-capades had me feeling sleepy. No wonder the temptation of Brandon's nice, big, clean bed was too much for me to resist; I immediately climbed up on it and made myself comfortable. By the time Eggy had finished dressing and turned around, I was already propped against the headboard with one of his pillows behind my back and the quilt pulled up over me.

"Make yourself comfortable, why don't you?" he snarked.

"Don't mind if I do," I replied with my bratty-best smile. "But I'd be much more comfortable if you joined me." I patted the spot next to me on the mattress. "Oh, and bring Billy's journal with you; we can read it together while we snuggle."

His nose scrunched up tightly as he looked at me in disgust. "I don't . . . snuggle," he insisted but at the same time he followed instructions by going out to the other room and grabbing the journal as I asked. When he returned, he had the object with him, keeping the book well away from his body and using a wet wipe to protect his fingers from the dusty cover. "Here. Just don't get dirt all over my fucking bed," he ordered before taking up his spot next to me.

To placate him, I used the wet wipe to remove any lingering dust, although it was already pretty clean after having most of the contamination wiped off by the fabric of my pants pocket on the trip back here through the tunnel. That small gesture seemed to appease the clean freak lying in bed with me, though, since he nodded approvingly when I looked in his direction. Accepting that as a general go ahead, I opened the front cover of the book and started reading the first entry aloud.

"January 1, 1885: 'Be at War with your Vices, at Peace with your Neighbours, and let every New-Year find you a better Man, or so says the esteemed Mr. Benjamin Franklin, and I have determined to make that my motto for this coming year in the hopes of ameliorating my condition. Father, I am sure, believes me incapable of such change, but I am resolved to prove him wrong. It needs only that I apply myself to my schooling, avoid temptation, and elect to choose wiser company, according to the paterfamilias. We shall see, I suppose. We shall see...'"

"Best laid plans of mice and men . . ." Brandon opined in response.

"Yeah, I'm pretty sure his father's idea of 'wiser company' probably didn't involve the type of men who frequented the Hotel Liberty," I agreed, picking up my phone off the side table where

I'd left it and pulling up the photos I'd taken of the secret barroom in the former Hotel's basement. "At least not the men who were using these little beauties . . ."

Brandon turned the screen towards himself so he could better see the pictures I'd taken of the drawers full of sex toys and whistled. "Wow! My, my, my . . . Those Victorian gay boys certainly liked their toys, it seems." I swiped through the pictures for him, allowing him to see the full panoply of all the goodies I'd discovered.

"You're not just kidding," I replied, getting to the picture of the device in the last drawer and enjoying the grimace the contraption caused on my Eggy's handsome face. "Anyone who was willing to take on THAT beast, was hardcore."

"I didn't even know S&M was a thing back then," Brandon voiced the same thought I'd had. "What's the rest of the room look like? Whips and chains hanging from the walls, no doubt?"

"Actually, no." I swiped through the pics again till I came to the shots I'd taken of the room itself. "It looked very elegant and presentable at first glance. Just like any other tavern of the time, I suppose. Except for the fact that this particular bar was hidden away in the basement, and there was no obvious door leading out to the Hotel proper, a casual observer wouldn't have any clue what went on there. Not until they looked in the cupboards, of course."

"No door?"

"Nope. Not that I could see. Although I suspect there was a secret entrance somewhere here, along this wall." I pointed out the spot on the picture I had taken showing the long wooden bar along the right-hand side of the room and then the empty space between that and the cupboards against the end wall. "See. They could have easily hidden a doorway like the one down in your basement over there."

"But why hide the room in the first place?" Brandon asked as he scrutinized the picture more thoroughly. "I mean, it was a Hotel, right? Which means that it would be perfectly normal to have a tavern on the premises. Why put the bar in the basement, in the first place, and then hide it with a secret door on top of everything?"

"Well, duh! Because it was GAY bar, of course," I answered. Brandon seemed skeptical, even though he'd seen the pictures of the dildos in the drawers. "Don't you see, Eggy? The Hotel was already getting called out by all the church folks, so they had to hide it! They were basically ALL in the closet back then."

"We don't know that they were ALL gay, Tristan."

"Well, enough of them were that they had a pretty impressive collection of things to shove up their asses." Brandon laughed at my phrasing and shrugged in concession. "Maybe Jones himself wasn't gay, but even if he was just willing to accommodate the clientele that swung that way because he was a good little capitalist, there's no reason to hide the whole room unless it really was specifically meant for his homosexual customers, right?" Brandon still didn't look like he was totally in agreement with me, so of course I sprang immediately into PSA mode. "Did you know that same sex sexual activity was technically illegal in Pennsylvania as late as 1980, when the sodomy laws were officially changed? Before that, it was illegal to have anal intercourse of any sort, even if it was between a married man and his wife. It was a felony, even. Hell, they were actually convicting people on those grounds as late as the seventies - there was this one serial killer who . . ."

"Are you minoring in Sodomy Studies or something, Brat? How do you know all this shit?" Egbert teased me, interrupting right when I was getting on a roll.

"Darla and I did a research project on the topic for Sociology back in Freshman year. It was really interesting, actually." He huffed a laugh or two at my nerdiness, causing me to blush, but still not shutting me up, because I don't shut up - or embarrass - that easily. "Anyway, the point is that, even if Jones himself wasn't gay, and was simply catering to his more deviant clients' interests, it was still illegal and he'd have wanted to hide the fact of what he was doing. And since there's no other explanation for wanting to hide the bar, ergo, it had to be what we today would call a 'gay bar'."

"I suppose it makes sense," Eggy finally conceded. "With all Jones' clients in the closet, why not put the closet itself out of sight in the basement. But that still doesn't explain why there's a tunnel between this building and the Hotel's 'gay bar'."

"Which is why I want to read this." I waved Billy's journal around triumphantly. "I'm hoping our boy Billy can solve the mystery." I opened the book again and started on the next entry.

"*. . . January 2nd, 1885: 'Father has asked me to join him at the Duquesne Club this afternoon for the weekly Commerce Committee meeting. I am dreading the tedium already. My resolutions for the New Year may already be in jeopardy . . .'*"

*****

Chapter 2

Dear Diary

"*January 15, 1885: 'I have survived another of the dreaded Commerce Committee meetings with my father. Today was worse than before, however, as Uncle Andrew was there and joined father in his lecturing about my life choices. I am beginning to suspect that they don't really wish me to amend my ways, elsewise they would have no one to vent their disapproval upon. So, not only was I forced to endure the tedium of more than an hour of incomprehensible facts and figures, but afterwards I was rewarded with a dose of the family's disapprobrium.'*" I continued to read aloud from Billy's journal.

"This kid whines a hell of a lot," Brandon commented from his spot beside me in the bed where we were snuggled up as we read the journal together. "Kind of like someone else I know," Brandon teased, giving me a gentle squeeze to let me know he was only kidding.

"Hey!" I scoffed, and gave him a little kick with my foot. Damn, I fucking loved being cuddled up with him like this. "But, yeah, he really does," I agreed, before I went back to my reading. "Oh, hey, this part gets more interesting . . . *'The only good thing about today's experience was that I was introduced to the newest member of the Committee, one Mr. Andrew Peebles. Peebles, it appears, is not only one of Our Fair City's preeminent architects, but also one of the men on my Uncle's short list to build the new Library he is contemplating for erection in Allegheny. I found Mr. Peebles to be exceedingly pleasant of manner and appearance . . .'"*

"'Pleasant of manner and appearance'?" Brandon echoed the words I'd just read. "Who the fuck talks like that? Just say he was hot and you wanted him to fuck the shit out of you, Billy. We all know that's what you were trying to say."

I swatted Brandon on the stomach with the back of my hand. "They didn't talk like that back then, you oaf. They were more . . . circumspect . . . especially if they were gay." Then I went back to my reading, excited that the next passage was more interesting still. *"'I have accepted the invitation of Mr. Peebles to join him for a glass of sherry this Friday at the Hotel Liberty and am greatly looking forward to engaging in more stimulating conversation about his architectural works . . .'"*

"Yeah, I'm sure he's real interested in Andy's newest 'Erection'," Brandon teased - making himself laugh - but then again, who among us doesn't get amused at the occasional erection joke, right?

We read through a few more entries of the journal, making fun of the stilted writing style and vague allusions to Billy's growing attraction to Andrew Peebles. But there wasn't anything concrete to get excited about in those first several entries. Before we were even through the third week of January, I was bored. It didn't help matters much that I was far too comfy and warm, lying there all cuddled up in Brandon's big bed. I was also still super tired after my week at the Diner. So it probably wasn't surprising that I soon began yawning so hard that it was difficult to tell what I was saying as I read. Soon enough, Brandon got annoyed by my antics and took over the reading for the both of us. Listening to his mellow, deep voice, droning on in the almost musical cadence of Billy's writing, however, didn't help keep me awake, and before long I felt my eyelids drooping.

When I woke up some time later, I discovered myself spooned up along Brandon's left side and my head pillowed by his broad chest as Brandon napped beside me. My pillow was breathing deeply, letting out an adorable little wheeze on every inhalation. I just laid there and listened to the pleasant rumbling for a while, more content than I can describe. This felt right. This was where I belonged. I fit here, both physically, with the way my body and his meshed together like two puzzle pieces and the way the hollow of his shoulder seemed just the right size for my head, but also emotionally. It felt like I'd found my happy place and it turned out to be a hundred year old building in the heart of Pittsburgh occupied by a hairy hermit. Who'da thunk it, huh?

While I was marvelling over my luck, the hermit in question moaned in his sleep and half rolled over so that his lower body was facing me, his long right leg hooking around my left calf. My head was still resting on Brandon's shoulder, but now I was being held even tighter to him, my nose pressed against the slightly sweaty skin of his collar bone. I inhaled happily, taking in the spicy aroma of his cologne mixed with sweat and whatever it was that was inherently him. It was a heady scent.

I instantly got horny.

Please don't judge me. I really couldn't help myself. I was so relaxed and comfy and warm and, by then, rested. My body was just open to any possibilities at that point. When he held me like that, and I was forced to breathe him in, it quickly became overwhelming. It didn't help matters much that my dick was now tightly trapped between our bodies, and every time I so much as inhaled it got jostled, providing a thrilling little shock of friction that only compounded the problem. So can you blame me if I indulged in a few minutes of gloriously decadent frotting?

Before long my activities came to the notice of my previously-slumbering bed mate; it was probably that last, rather vocal, moan that I couldn't completely stifle. Brandon awoke with a groan of his own and then, with my next thrust against his hip, he used the heel hooked behind my calf to pull me around, rolling us together until I was perched on top of him, our full bodies touching with only the thin material of our sweatpants separating us. So we frotted and squirmed together and eventually our lips made contact allowing us to add kissing into the mix and fuck me if I wasn't just about going insane with lust by that point. It was fucking glorious!

Thank fuck for that tiny little voice of caution in the back of my mind, though. It kept telling me, over and over, that I couldn't take this any further, no matter what my dick was telling me. For once I even listened to that voice of reason - which I think shows tremendous personal growth, don't you? - pulling back right before things got to the 'point of no return' stage.

"I think . . . I think we . . . we better . . . slow down . . . a bit," I panted, working hard to get my brain back online sufficiently to get actual words out. "Won't be able . . . able to stop . . . if . . ."

"Who said I want you to stop," Brandon pointed out, towing my face back down so he could reach my lips again, and canting his hips upwards so that his erection ground against my own in the most delicious manner.

Good point. Why was I trying to stop these wonderful feelings again? What was that we'd been saying earlier about interesting erections? "Mmmmm . . . Okay . . . Kissing good . . ."

But even then that nagging piece of my conscience wouldn't let up completely. It kept bugging me, telling me that Brandon might WANT to continue, but he wasn't READY for the results. With what little was left of my rational processes, I scrambled to come up with some alternative that would work. Something that would allow us to keep on keeping on but without triggering my boyfriend's OCD. There had to be some way to make us both happy.

Then, out of the corner of my eye, I spied the huge organizer tray full of condoms Brandon had sitting on the nightstand next to his bed. Leave it to Egbert to have organized even his condom supply, right? He couldn't just have random half-full boxes of them stashed in some drawer like every other man in America; no, Eggy had a special, stainless steel, three-troughed, wire-mesh tray, with all his condoms perfectly lined up, every one of them facing the same way, the lines exactly even except for the first one in each row, which was slightly elevated above the rest as if waiting to be plucked free. So, of course my mind went right to, 'why not?'.

Without breaking our kiss, I freed my left hand and pulled out the first one of the bunch. Of course, then I had to free my other hand in order to tear open the package, but I still managed to maintain a solid lip lock on Eggy's mouth while I accomplished this step. In fact, it wasn't until I began to reach between our bodies, squirming and wiggling around so that I could make enough room to reach my crotch, that Brandon seemed to twig to what I was doing.

"Tristan . . . I don't know if I can . . ." Brandon mumbled, the vibrations of his words felt against my own lips as he spoke.

"I know," I replied, adding a kiss of reassurance at the end. "Do you trust me?"

"Yes," he replied without any hesitation at all, and fuck me, if that didn't make me hornier than I already was.

I gave him one more kiss, biting at his bottom lip with a tug as I pulled away, and then sat up so that I was straddling him. With Eggy watching, I unearthed my cock from the baggy sweatpants. I then very deliberately rolled the condom I'd already opened down its length. Brandon was watching my every move with a hungry smile. Next, I grabbed another condom and, just as deliberately, reached out towards the waist of his matching sweats. For a split second I thought he was going to stop me, his hand darting out as if he was going to pull my hand away, but instead, he just gripped my wrist tightly as I reached inside and pulled out his beautiful dick. I wanted more than anything to take him into my mouth and suck him dry, but instead I did what I'd originally planned to do, and rolled a second condom down his length.

I had seen his dick before, held it in my hand even, but I had been so busy giving the hand job of my life that I'd never noticed just how ... big ... he actually was. I'm not talking length here - yes he was a solid nine or so inches, I remembered that much - but the girth on that thing was pretty phenomenal. Just thinking of what he could do to me with that instrument had me groaning out loud and rubbing my ass furiously against his legs like some depraved animal.

Brandon grinned up at me as he settled himself against a pillow and shuffled down the bed a bit until he was where he wanted us. His hands gripped my waist and I felt him bring his knees up so that I had something to lean against.

I looked down at our cocks, which were resting rather heavily together and I signed happily.

"So, what? You just going to sit there all day contemplating how amazing our dicks look together? Or are you going to show me what you're made of, Brat?" Brandon asked smugly.

I totally wasn't prepared for that much assertiveness so I sat there, on his lap, with my mouth wide open, until the hands on my waist gripped me tighter and he began moving me against him.

"Imagine you're riding me, Tristan," he ordered in this sex-heavy voice that went straight to my groin.

His words caused my dick to become painfully hard but I knew

I wanted, more than anything, to make this good for Brandon, so I had to restrain myself. I shuffled a little closer up his body and then leaned forward so I could rest my hands on either side of the pillow he was laying against. I began gyrating my hips, rocking back and forth - his cock rubbing along the crack of my ass and mine trapped between our stomachs - never breaking eye contact with him. Before I knew what was going on, Brandon had manhandled me to where he wanted me and was controlling our movements with strong, self-assured, and forceful movements. He knew exactly what he was doing and, more importantly, what he wanted.

All I can say is, if I had died right then, I would have died one very happy and satisfied man.

Brandon's body began jerking wildly underneath me as he got closer and closer. The almost silent puffs of air he let out would be forever ingrained in my brain, like a favorite song. I closed my eyes so I could focus more intently on the delicious noises he was making. Damn, he was providing me with so much jerk off material, that I might never leave my bed again . . . Well, only to do this again right here in his bed.

"Look at me, Tristan."

I obliged, opening my eyes again and shivering as I stared into his lust-darkened pupils.

"I want you looking at me when you cum. I want to watch it in your eyes. I want to see the exact moment you lose yourself to me."

Those fucking words and the pressure of his hard cock grating against my ass as I rocked back and forth was what finally pushed me over the edge. I felt myself exploding from somewhere deep inside, a wash of fire flowing through every nerve ending, and my body shaking violently as my orgasm took over. I literally couldn't see straight. I knew I was still looking into

Brandon's eyes, but I saw nothing but a bright white light. At the same time, I felt the body under mine bucking and heard a groan that matched my own, only in a deeper tone, before Brandon too finally came to a panting stop.

When my vision finally cleared, I found myself collapsed on top of Brandon's chest, huffing like I'd run a fucking marathon. Out of the corner of my eye I could see my Apple Watch flashing brightly, alerting me to my unusually high heart rate. Shit, 201 bpm? Good thing I was young and not genetically prone to heart attacks, or else shit like that would kill me, I thought with a quiet chuckle.

Maybe in response to my jollity, or maybe just because he wanted to, Brandon took that opportunity to wrap his arms around me, holding me so tightly I felt enveloped. Not that I was gonna object; I'd never felt so cared for ever in my life. I could hear Eggy's heart beating loudly against my ear - almost as loudly as my own - and I turned my head and dropped a kiss on his sweaty chest. He tasted salty and delicious and I wished I could bottle that taste and save it forever.

"Fuck, Brandon. That was…" I didn't have the right words to finish that sentence so I gave up halfway through.

"You have . . ." Brandon waited a second so he could catch his breath before continuing, ". . . no idea . . . how much I wanted that . . . Tristan."

I rubbed myself teasingly against his already re-hardening cock, "I have a slight idea," I grinned.

After about a half a minute more of just panting in tandem, I reached over to the nightstand, grabbed a handful of tissues, lifted myself up, and reached into my sweats so I could pull off my condom. Brandon did the same. I grabbed them both, holding them up to judge the volume of the contents, and gave my Egbert an approving look.

"Fucking hell, Brandon! You shoot more than a . . . I don't know . . . more than a blue whale probably."

He shook his head at my juvenile remarks and then made this disgusted face, probably grossed out by my playing around with the icky, used condoms. Not wanting to trigger him and ruin the moment, I hurried to wrap them both in tissues, making sure not to spill anything. He looked on, approvingly, as I tossed the wad I'd made towards the trash can, smiling proudly at me as I made a perfect basket. Then I moved around so I could once more assume my comfy spot, curled up like a contented cat next to him in bed.

"Mmmm. I like it here," I confessed, letting my hand drift upwards so I could play with the long hairs of his beard, creating a series of perfect little curly pyramidal structures. "This feels . . . safe . . . you know?"

My Eggy made this happy mumbling sound in agreement. The noise reverberated through his chest and caused me to smile. I buried my face deeper into the crook of his neck so I could breathe in his musky, sweaty goodness.

Which is when I realized I truly liked the people we were when we were together - and I know that sounds moronically stupid to say, but it's the truth - we were good for each other in ways I'd never even thought about before meeting Brandon. I wondered about that for a bit, and how lucky it was that I seemed to have found my person, after all the false starts and superficial relationships I'd tried in the past. I wondered if that was the way it was for everyone. Were all those romance novels right? Did you just KNOW when it was meant to be?

While I was waxing philosophical in my crowded and busy head, I spied Billy's discarded journal which was lying halfway buried under Brandon's pillow. He must have dropped it when we fell asleep earlier and it got shoved aside by our happy-time antics. But thinking about Billy and Andrew, in the afterglow of our lovemaking, got me wondering again. Was Andrew the one true love of young William Carnegie? Was it like that for them? What would that journal tell me?

I reached over and grabbed the book without moving from my spot lying with my head on Brandon's chest, and flipped to the page where we'd left off. I briefly scanned through a couple more mundane entries. Then I found something juicy and decided to read it aloud to my bed mate.

"Listen to this," I told Brandon as I recited the interesting journal entry I'd discovered. "'*January 21, 1885: 'Last night I joined Mr. Andrew Peebles for the libation that he had earlier invited me to share and, may I say, the experience was enlightening. I met Mr. Peebles (or, as he implored me to call him by his given name, Andrew) at the Club, after which he escorted me to the Hotel Liberty, a well known establishment just a block or so away, whereupon he introduced me to his circle of friends. As several of the gentlemen were already known to me, I was quickly put at ease in their company. The owner of the hotel, Mr. BF Jones (also known as 'Beefy' to his more intimate acquaintances) soon invited a select few of us to accompany him to his private rooms in the basement of the building. Andrew and I followed the rest and were made right at home. We proceeded to play cards and drink far more Brandy than was probably good for us, causing me to become downright giddy before very long. That is likely the reason I did not take notice of the other activities going on around me until things had gotten rather scandalous. I daren't detail all the happenings that occured, not even in the sacrosanct confines of my personal journal, for fear of discovery, but suffice it to say that I was soon exposed to things I had never thought to imagine. I fear that, should I continue my association with Andrew and his provocative friends, I shall never succeed in turning over that 'new leaf' my father wished for me this year.'*'"

"Sounds like young Billy had a busy night," Brandon surmised with a sexy smirk.

"If he was introduced to all the toys 'Beefy' kept in his base-ment, you can count on it," I agreed. "You know . . . when I was doing my project on your building, I looked up Peebles' history and, by the time he was building this place, he was pretty old. Like fifty or something. Which means that there was a huge age gap between him and Billy. Which is . . . kinda creepy, you know, especially if he was taking a kid like that to wild orgies and all."

"You have a problem with older men, Kid?"

I laughed. "Of course not, but it's not like you're THAT old. Or, maybe you are, and the beard just hides it? I don't know . . ."

"Bite your tongue, youngling," Egbert ordered with a playful squeeze of my shoulders from that arm wrapped around me. "Besides, from the sounds of it, your Billy was already well on his way to debauchery before he even met Peebles. Why else would his father have been lecturing him about 'turning over a new leaf' and all? I don't suppose Peebles showed the boy any-thing he didn't already want to know."

"Maybe. But I don't think their relationship could have been all that strong, what with the huge disparity in their ages," I con-cluded, answering my own prior musings. "I mean, if you went by what Peebles wrote in that love letter we found behind the picture, you'd think they were lovers for a lot longer than what this journal says. They'd only met in January and by May he was dedicating the building to him? It was either a whirlwind ro-mance or just a crazy infatuation on Peebles' part."

Brandon's only answer was tapping on the edge of the journal I was still holding, indicating that I would likely find my answers, if they existed, in the book.

I went back to reading. There were the usual boring daily entries - Billy had been quite the diligent journaler - but it was mostly about unimportant family issues and meetings his father made him attend as Thomas tried to groom his son to eventually take over the family business. None of it made much of an impression on me. However, a couple of weeks after the entry where Billy had first gone to the Hotel Liberty, there was another entry specific to Peebles.

"*February 3, 1885: 'Andrew is taking me to see the progress on his building today. He is rightfully proud to be the architect and owner of such an imposing edifice. He tells me it will be done later this year, of which he is glad, as he is eager to take up his next challenge. I have promised to report favorably on the work's progress to my Uncle in the hopes that it will propel Andrew higher in Uncle's consideration for his Library project. A job such as that would be quite the feather in my Andrew's professional cap and I shall do whatever I can to win him the honor.'*"

"Makes you wonder what they got up to while Peebles was giving him the tour of the building, huh? What's that old saw, 'wanna come up to my place and see my etchings?'" I joked, enjoying laughing together with my Eggy.

"If these walls could talk . . ."

We continued to read through the journal as the afternoon settled into evening and the weak winter sun set outside the warm confines of Eggy's Tower. I didn't care. I would gladly never move again if I didn't have to. It didn't hurt to have something interesting to occupy my thoughts as I was lolling around in Brandon's arms, though, and this journal was definitely proving to be that.

"Damn! Looks like Billy's father got wise to what he was up to at the Hotel Liberty," I read in a subsequent entry. "Listen to this . . . '*March 8, 1885: I have had a horrible row with Father this morning and am terribly distraught. That old busybody, Reverend Clarke, and his Presbyters, have again been raising a stink over what they view as the rampant lawlessness and sin of Our Fair City. These annoying do-gooders went so far as to send a delegation to confront the City Council, wherein the Reverend called out several of what he calls 'Dens of Iniquity'. Unfortunately, both Father and Uncle happened to be in attendance at that meeting, and were appalled to discover that the Hotel Liberty, a place I have been frequenting often over the past month or so, is included on the good Reverend's list of places he wants eradicated. I was henceforth subjected to the familiar lecture about how I am seen as a representative of 'The Family' and I must mind my reputation for fear of sullying theirs . . . etcetera, etcetera, etcetera. In the end, I was threatened with financial ruin if I was ever again seen entering the doors of the dreaded establishment. But if I am forbidden that refuge, wherever shall Andrew and I find another safe haven?'"*

"Looks like Billy got caught being naughty," Brandon summed up the entry in his usual curt way.

"Yeah. Poor guy. I feel for him. I remember living with a homophobic father and having to sneak out of the house all the time back when I was in high school. It wasn't fun. But a gay boy has to do what a gay boy has to do, right?"

Brandon shrugged. "At least until he gets caught and his father threatens to cut him off from his older lover."

"We know that's not the whole story, though," I replied. "If it had been, we never would have found that May love letter. They must have found some way to be together, despite Billy's dad."

Luckily, I didn't have to read much further to discover just how it was that our lovers had managed their ongoing tryst. In the process, I also came across the answer to one of the more puzzling parts of our building's mystery: why the hidden tunnels?

"March 15, 1885: My dear Andrew is such a clever fellow; I shall never doubt him again. He has solved all our problems with his architectural genius. When I came to him, in despair over the fallout from my discussions with Father and Uncle, he went right to work devising a solution and came up with the perfect expedient. Andrew posited that the real solution was NOT that I must now begin

frequenting less disreputable venues than the Hotel Liberty and any other such 'Reprobate Establishments', but that I should henceforth avoid being SEEN to go to these places. According to his brilliant, unconventional mind, all that was needed was a mechanism by which I could continue to join him in our usual haunts, while accessing those places via some alternative entrance. And, in mere days, he has designed me just such a contrivance! It seems that the City of Pittsburgh has already been working to facilitate our plans; they have been installing improved plumbing, sewer and gas lines throughout the downtown area by way of excavation of several utility tunnels beneath our very sidewalks, and Andrew has assured me that we can take advantage of this fact. Accordingly, he is already constructing a special tunnel, making use of the City's existing utility excavations, to connect his new building to the Hotel Liberty. This proposed underground entrance should allow us to access all the amusements offered by Dear Beefy, without fear of detection. As I said, the man is a genius!"'

"Aha!" I exclaimed when I'd finished reading that particular passage. "That's the reason for the tunnels! They were put in so Billy and his lover could continue to hang out at their favorite gay club! See? Life back then really wasn't that different than it is today; gay boys have always had to hide from their fathers."

"Only, back then, instead of secretly texting their older gay lovers, they had to build entire secret tunnels," Eggy pointed out.

"Well, yeah. They did kinda go all out there, huh?

"Ya think?" Brandon laughed, whether at me or at the image of Peebles building Billy secret tunnels, wasn't really important.

"Good thing all I had to do to be with MY older gay lover was break into his building," I concluded.

"That is a good thing," Eggy agreed with me.

Then he knocked the journal I'd been reading out of my hands so he could roll over on top of me and distract me from any further reading by taking possession of my lips with his own.

*****

Chapter 3

Chocolate

I stayed over at Eggy's again that night, only this time I wasn't relegated to the guest room, and that made all the difference in the world. We read some more in Billy's journal, we talked, we kissed and, before we finally settled down for the night, we once again did our sorta, kinda, partially clothed and fully suited up, sex thing. Don't judge! It worked for us and that was all that mattered.

Unfortunately, my winter break was over and I had to go back to school again the following morning. It was probably for the best, though, because Eggy needed to work too and we couldn't spend ALL our time in bed together. I wish! Anyway, I headed off to class, ready to start in on a whole new term of projects and fun while Egbert headed to his office for the day.

I was more than happy with my new classes. The Graphic Design course I'd signed up for was going to be fun, as was the print-making class, but it was the Painting Processes class that I was really looking forward to, even though it would probably be the most challenging. For my core classes, I was taking History of the Renaissance as well as Modern Poetry, both of which should be relatively easy As for me as I'd had similar classes in High

School.

In between my classes, I continued to read through Billy's Journal. The entries were definitely beginning to heat up as the year progressed. Throughout March and into April, Peebles' name began to show up more and more often. Reading between the lines, I could tell that Andrew was wooing Billy pretty hard. And, maybe I was reading too much into the narrative because of my own bias, but it seemed to me like Billy was reluctant to accept all of Andrew's overtures, even though he was obviously enjoying all the new and likely eye-opening experiences that being Andrew's acolyte afforded. Reading about it all, though, felt a bit like reading some Victorian romance novel, what with all the veiled yet steamy references to sex. If Billy was getting laid even half as much as he alluded to, that boy must have been busy.

I was immersed in reading another such passage while I chowed down on my lunch in the TAIP cafeteria when my romantic fantasies were interrupted by the arrival of a group of friends who came to join my table. I happily made room for them, clearing away my drawing pad and the random pencils I'd left scattered around, and set Billy's journal aside as well. It wasn't until Patrick and Connor took up their seats across from me that I noticed Zeboria, the third member of the group, wasn't alone. Zee was accompanied by none other than my old stalker, Ian Golding. What made it even worse was, by the time Z took a seat next to Connor, the only chair left at our table was the one right next to me.

"Hey, Tee, you know Ian, right?" Zeboria introduced us, oblivious to the disdainful look I was already shooting the musician.

"Yeah, we've met," I responded tersely without even gracing the newcomer seated beside me with so much as a glance.

Ian returned the favor, ignoring me back, which was fine with me actually. I had nothing to say to him. But it probably wasn't surprising that I didn't stick around for long after that. I just didn't feel comfortable around Ian any more, especially knowing his propensity for reading some tacit hint of attraction into my every action. I had just barely managed to get him to back off after our blow up, and the last thing I needed was for him to mistakenly think I'd changed my mind. So I soon scarfed down what was left of my lunch, said goodbye to my friends, and made my escape. Since it was almost time for me to get to my Poetry class, I went straight to that classroom and killed the time until the professor arrived by reading more from Billy's journal.

After class was over, I rushed away from campus as fast as I could. I know I'd only just left Egbert's a few hours earlier, but I was almost desperate to get back to him. Young love and all, right? While I was waiting for the bus, however, I noticed how horribly chapped my lips were - collateral damage from all the kissing Brandon and I had been doing lately, I suppose - and decided to pop into the corner pharmacy to get some lip balm. I needed to have soft, supple, kissable lips for my Eggy, right?

Probably due to the horribly cold weather Pittsburgh had been suffering through, the display for my favorite type of lip balm - Burt's Bees - was empty. I asked the clerk if he had more and he agreed to go check for me in the back. While I was waiting, I ambled around the store, perusing the shelves, only half paying attention to what I was seeing since my mind was still caught up in the story from Billy's journal.

It wasn't until my rambling took me down the aisle where they kept the 'intimate personal care' items that I started to pay attention. This particular pharmacy, which was right off Liberty Avenue, seemed to have a larger than normal stock of these items. There was everything a gay man or woman might need: special soaps for intimate places, gels and creams with uses I didn't want to think about, and about a dozen different kinds of hemorrhoid cures. There was also a whole section dedicated solely to lubricants. Who even knew there were that many types of lube? I longingly looked at a few of the more interesting offerings, but knew it was gonna be quite some time before Eggy and I would need that. However, right next to the lubes was another display of items the two of us could put to use right away - condoms!

I enthusiastically scanned through the truly impressive selection the store carried; there were just so many fun options! I quickly skipped over all the ribbed and textured types, because we weren't ready for that yet, before I came across several kinds of flavored condoms. That gave me a wickedly decadent idea and I immediately picked out two boxes. Luckily, the clerk returned ten seconds later with my lip balm and I was off, fully supplied with everything I'd need for Eggy's next big adventure!

Twenty minutes later I was kicking at the lobby door of Brandon's building, my hands filled with our usual coffee drinks, and my mind occupied with this evening's plans for my hermit's delectable body. Brandon and Bill were both galloping down the stairs a half a minute later and each looked happy to see me. I almost didn't have time to open Bill's creamer before Bill's person grabbed my hand and started towing me up the stairs so fast I almost fell over my own feet. I guess Brandon was just as eager to see me as I was to see him.

As soon as we reached Brandon's room on the top floor, he towed me over to the couch and pulled me down into his lap. It's not like I was gonna object or anything, but the urgency of his actions was kinda sweet. Before I knew what hit me, his lips had suctioned themselves to my own and we were right back where we'd left off earlier that morning.

I seriously can't remember the last time I had actually sat down and made out with someone for so long. Things had definitely progressed between Brandon and I; we kissed practically every time we saw each other, we regularly participated in deliciously wet handjobs in the shower, and then last night we'd more or less fucked with our clothes on. It was the closest his dick had ever gotten to my ass, and damn it had felt good. If you had told me a few months ago that I would get off from dry humping a hot guy, with a condom and pair of sweats between us, I would have laughed in your face. But somehow it ended up being one of the hottest and most intense sexual experiences of my life. Hell, if and when we actually do get to fuck, I'll probably die from the pleasure of it all. Anyway, that experience already felt like too long ago - what with a whole school day in the middle and all - so I was more than happy, as soon as I arrived at my Eggy's tower that afternoon, to be greeted with a good old fashioned kiss-a-thon.

"I love kissing you," I whispered, as I pulled back slightly and rubbed our noses together like some love sick fool, which caused Brandon to shake his head and laugh at me, before he pulled me back in for some more wet, open-mouthed lip locking.

At some point in the proceedings I felt Brandon scoot back a little in his seat on the couch and bring one of his legs up onto the sofa. He then moved me so I was sitting in between his thighs, my legs draped over the tops of his. I loved being surrounded by him like that. His dick was already rock hard and pressing against the fly of his jeans and it reminded me of the little present I had picked up on my way over. I couldn't wait to get started on the experiment I had planned; I hoped I wasn't pushing things with Brandon, but if he let me . . . Fuck, I couldn't even think about what I would do if he agreed. Or, for that matter, what I'd do if he didn't agree.

"What's up?" Eggy asked as he felt me pull back and reach for my bag that I'd dumped on the floor next to the sofa.

I felt for the box with my hand and threw it into Brandon's lap, making sure that I watched his face carefully to see what sort of reaction this little gift of mine would make.

He scrunched his nose up and looked at me. "Flavored condoms?"

"Sooo, here's what I was thinking," I replied quickly as I didn't want Eggy to start jumping to conclusions in his head the way I knew he would. "I love your cock," I told him honestly.

I smiled over at him and reached down, making sure to give him a nice, firm squeeze through his jeans. The feeling of his dick swelling through the material was almost enough for me to lose my train of thought. I think I made my point though.

"Really? I would never guess," he groaned quietly, smiling back as he continued teasing me, his body subconsciously moving further down the sofa cushions so that he was practically slouching. "You should make it more obvious."

"Well, funny you should say that, because I was thinking . . ." I picked the box back up and bit down nervously on the cardboard. I wasn't sure what I was nervous about exactly, because I wanted this, it's just that I wanted Brandon to want it as much as me.

". . ." He gestured with his hand, indicating that I should continue talking.

Like the smooth guy that I am, however, I ended up just blurting it out. "I want to suck you off."

Brandon's eyebrows shot up into his hairline.

"Tristan . . . I don't know if I . . ."

There went that damn brain of his again; I wish it would mind its own fucking business.

"Just listen to me, 'kay?" I asked, placing my hand back on his denim clad dick.

Brandon nodded and nudged my hand to continue its exploring.

"I know this might not be something you're ready to do on me . . . yet . . . and I'm totally okay with that," I assured him. "But I thought maybe with a condom on you might be alright with me doing it to you."

I watched as he took in everything I had said, his tongue nestled deep into his cheek as though he was seriously contemplating my proposal.

"So, why the flavors?"

I shrugged. "I thought it would be fun."

"Are you saying sucking my plain flavored, condom-covered dick would be boring?" The asshole was smirking. But did this mean he was okay with my plan?

"Yeah, who wants plain and boring, when you can have . . ." I turned the box over and read through the selection contained within, picking out one flavor at random. "Bubblegum."

"No." He shook his head in disgust.

"Oooh, cake batter." I licked my lips and ripped open the box, giving it a quick sniff.

"You are not making my dick taste like a fucking birthday cake." It was quite funny how appalled he actually looked.

I wrinkled my nose at the next one. "Ewww, bacon?"

"Well, it IS a tasty piece of meat . . ."

I threw my head back and laughed. It didn't matter how much I loved bacon, that was definitely not the one I would be picking. "Okay, if you're not up for one of the more exotic flavors, that leaves either chocolate or vanilla . . . I think I'm going to go with vanilla," I smiled at my choice.

"I think I object to my cock being called 'vanilla'," Eggy protested with a shake of his head.

"Fine. Sheesh. For someone who wasn't sure he even wanted to do this, you're sure bossy," I complained, pulling the one last non-objectionable flavor out of the box and trailing the scratchy edge of the packaging down his abs. "That leaves only chocolate. Is that acceptable to you, Mr. Picky?"

"I suppose." He shrugged. "I mean, I'm not THAT bothered; pick whatever you want."

I easily saw through his pretend indifference. His already hard dick was now straining at the restriction of his jeans, making the fabric pull against the buttons. My guy was just as excited about the prospect of this new permutation as I was. Which meant it was time to move things along here.

I made short work of those buttons, opening the fly of his jeans, pulling his briefs down, and releasing the beast within. Damn, I wasn't just kidding about how much I had come to love his dick. Once freed, it stood there, sprouting from the center of a bed of curly, dark auburn pubes, projecting upwards, tall and proud, the color an almost angry mauve except for the lighter-colored cap, and the texture all smooth, silk-covered steel. My mouth literally watered as I looked at it. I wanted to take him between my lips and taste him so badly. So bad in fact that I had to reach into my pants and give myself a hard squeeze to try and ease some of the pressure in my own dick.

It was a temptation too strong to resist, even though I knew Eggy wasn't completely there yet, but I just HAD to bend down and leave one, tiny, closed-mouthed kiss right on the leaking tip. Even that small transgression was too much for him, though, and I felt him shift away from me. I had to rein myself in; I wanted to do this right for him, and for me, not cause him distress. So, before I could get myself into trouble, I quickly tore open the condom packet with my teeth, extracted the chocolate-brown piece of latex, and immediately began rolling it over the object of my attentions. I felt Brandon relax slightly the second I started. Oh well, I'd have to set aside my fantasies about tasting him for another time. Still, I managed to lick my lips surreptitiously while Brandon's eyes were closed, savoring the small sample of his jizz that remained from my kiss, and told myself I could wait for more.

I didn't have the leisure of dwelling in my fantasies for long, though - I had a task to accomplish - so I re-focused my attention on the work in front of me. I finished sheathing him up and then resituated myself so I was kneeling on the floor between his wide spread knees. I made a few passes with my hand up and down his length just to renew his hard on and then it was go time. I slowly leaned forward, trying to eke out the anticipation a little longer, teasing him by hovering just millimeters from making contact, and causing him to cant his hips upward in frustration. I capitulated with a chuckle, opening wide and letting my lips slide down, over the swollen head, past the ridge at the bottom of the flared cap, and then further still, until I felt his dick tickling against the back of my palate. I hummed approvingly and pulled back just far enough so my tongue could circle around him, licking at the chocolatey tasting condom with approval. It wasn't bad. I would have still loved tasting him raw instead, but until that happened, this was acceptable.

"Mmmmm. That feels so . . . oh, fuck, Tristan," Brandon started to moan and babble as I set to work for real. He was pulling at my hair with both hands as if searching for a real handhold. I loved that I seemed able to break through the stoic front he usually tried to maintain. The more I sucked and licked and hummed around his dick, the more vocal my stylite became. "Shit! More . . . More . . . There, yes . . . Oh, fuck . . ."

It really didn't take long at all. In less than ten minutes I could tell he was ready to shoot. I began to massage his balls with one hand while I snaked the other up his chest, twisting one perky nipple for added effect. I could hear the uptick in his rate of breathing and feel the way his body was practically vibrating.

I was almost getting off just listening to his joyful little moans and gurgles. Then there was the familiar moment when it all came together; his balls contracted and the cock in my mouth bucked as I sucked him as deeply as I could go. I felt him shaking through his orgasm, the reservoir at the tip of the condom filling and heating up, and then he slumped backwards like his bones had all melted in the conflagration.

I sat back and smiled smugly up at him. "Proud of yourself?" he asked.

"Exceedingly!" I winked, before reaching into my bag and pulling out some napkins I'd grabbed with that afternoon's coffee run. I then carefully peeled the condom off of Brandon, making sure nothing leaked, and patted him clean with my napkins. Once the condom was wrapped up and safely out of sight I couldn't help but ask, despite knowing full well I was a solid 10, because if there's one thing I exceed at in this world, it's sucking cock, but still, I was curious . . . "So, how did I do?"

"Brat!"

"Shut up. You know you love my bratty side." I laughed heartily as I reached down and began to pull his boxers and jeans back up for him. Brandon helped out by lifting his ass up without me even having to ask, demonstrating just how comfortable the man had become with our escapades. I was training him so well. I then crawled up and made myself comfortable on his lap, curling around him like a needy kitten.

"May I help you?" He asked, smiling one of the biggest smiles I had ever seen from him.

"I'm hungry," I blurted out. Sometimes I swear I have no control over what I'm about to say.

"You just ate," he chuckled.

"Eating your cock doesn't count, even if it did taste like chocolate. I need real carbs, damn it!" I insisted. "Actually, I need chocolate. Ooooo, I know! I want some M&Ms! Your choco-cock gave me a craving."

"I don't keep that shit in my house."

I exhaled dramatically. "I know. Which means I'm going to have to venture out and get something. I may die of hunger otherwise."

Reluctantly I climbed down off his comfy lap and sighed. I noticed the abandoned coffees sitting on the nearby table. They were obviously cold by that point and basically inedible. So much for my coffee-based-OCD therapy for that afternoon.

Brandon must have noticed the direction of my gaze as he offered a sort of apology. "I didn't mean to distract you and waste your coffee."

"No problem, it was definitely worth it! Anyway, I can get more if I'm going out for chocolate."

He seemed sheepish, "I'd offer to pay but I don't actually have any cash in the house . . ." He looked uncomfortable for a minute but then bravely finished what he had been going to say. ". . . paper money kinda grosses me out anyway. Too many people touch it. It's better to just buy over the internet, you know?"

"I know, Eggy," I reassured him that I understood with a squeeze to his shoulder. "But no worries. I have a punch card somewhere in here." I pulled the item out of the front pocket of my bag triumphantly. "See. Since I've already bought you 10 drinks, the next one is even free!"

"Frugal," he conceded.

"You forget, I'm a starving artist. I have to pinch pennies," I explained. Before heading to the door, though, I remembered the other thing besides the flavored condoms that I'd been excited to share with my hermit that day, and fished Billy's journal out of my bag as well. "While I'm gone, you should check out the entries for the beginning of May. There's some interesting things going on in your building in those entries."

Brandon used a couple of tissues to take the book out of my hand and then I was off to scavenge myself some sugar and caffeine to tide me over till dinner.

When I came back about half an hour later, a bag full of junk food and two fresh coffees in my hands, Brandon was still on the sofa where I'd left him, the journal in his lap, and a thoughtful look on his handsome face.

"Found anything good?" I asked, handing him the Chai Tea I'd bought him, which he took right off the bat without any hesitation at all, my brave boy!

Brandon seemed too engrossed in what he was reading to even notice that he'd taken a sip of the tea. I silently thrilled at the progress we were making. Not that I would ever say anything, because why jinx it, right? I was glad to see that he seemed to like the chai, though, judging by the way he stopped after that first taste, took a deeper sniff at the steam wafting out of the hole in the lid, and then tried another, larger, sip. It seemed we had a winner in the drinks department.

"I found the entry for the day Peebles finished the building," Brandon advised, setting aside the drink to raise the book he'd been reading. "*May 6, 1885: Today was the celebration marking the completion of my dear Andrew's building. It is a truly exemplary edifice; the bold triangular design, the noble architecture, not to mention the fact that it is now the tallest structure in the vicinity, all make it stand out from the more menial buildings that surround it. I could not be prouder of Andrew and was gratified to have been included amongst those at the ribbon cutting to commemorate the occasion. I am obviously not alone in these sentiments either, if the turn out for the Opening Day Ceremonies are anything to judge by; at times the gathering looked more like a City Council meeting than a party. I also finally met Andrew's partner - the heretofore mysteri- ous and faceless J. Frick - who attended the festivities with his wife, Alma. Mr. Frick was quite solicitous and charming, doing his best to make one and all feel appreciated, all while working diligently to find takers for the remaining offices that are as yet unlet. I was en- tirely won over by the man, so much so that I allowed myself to be persuaded to accept an invitation to take tea with the Fricks next Tuesday . . ."*

Brandon handed the journal over to me so I could scan the entry myself as he added, "Looks like Peebles better watch out; his boy has what they would have called back then, 'a wandering eye'."

I shrugged. "Maybe, but Frick was married - we know that from the history book you have in your office - so I doubt Peebles was too worried."

"Married, but obviously not above cheating on said wife. Be- sides, he wouldn't be the first gay man to have a wife and family. Weren't you the one talking about how closeted they all were back then? A wife can make a great beard, you know," Brandon hypothesized.

By that point I'd already flopped down on the sofa next to my Eggy and ripped into the bag of M&Ms I'd brought back with me. Brandon gave me a look that probably had something to do with the fact I was eating with my hands right out of the bag, but I figured it was good for him to constantly push his limits, so I just carried on. Meanwhile, I skimmed over the next few entries of Billy's memoir until I found another interesting one.

"Hmm. You may be right, Eggy. Listen to this: *'May 11, 1885: Andrew and I joined Mr. Frick and his wife for tea this evening. It was an eminently pleasant experience. Mrs. Frick is an accomplished artist and took the occasion to present her husband and his partner with a lovely drawing she had done of the completed building."* So that answers the mystery of who drew that picture of the building at least; I guess the second name started with an 'F' after all," I commented before delving back into the journal. "'*Andrew vowed to hang this wonderful piece of art in a place of prominence, the Boardroom, which greatly pleased the artist. The evening was only marred when Mrs. Frick was forced to excuse herself on account of a troublesome bout of neuralgia. However, after our female companion withdrew, we men took ourselves off to Andrew's basement hideaway for more manly pursuits than tea (composed mostly of cigars and brandy). I was loathe to agree to this relocation at first, fearful of the reaction Andrew and I might get from Frick, but was quickly dissuaded from my trepidation. Frick proved perfectly convivial and accepting of our special arrangement. He assured me, repeatedly, that he and Andrew had an understanding and, although he himself was a married man, he had no antipathy towards those of us inclined towards perpetual bachelorhood. And so the evening passed in happy comradeship.*'"

"Well, at least he wasn't a homophobe," Brandon concluded.

"If Frick and Peebles were business partners, I suppose Frick would have had to know something was off about Andrew. I wonder how Alma felt about all that, though? Based on that letter she wrote Jay, I'd say she was a lot less open minded than her husband."

"Or maybe it was just the adultery thing rather than the gay thing," Brandon suggested. "I hear women are kinda uptight about that shit?"

I laughed because Eggy's take on things was so warped sometimes - especially since he knew nothing about women whatsoever - but his skewed perspective was one of the reasons I loved him. I liked being shown the world from a different point of view. I liked trying to figure him out. I liked the challenge of him. Fuck, I'm so pathetic, aren't I? Oh well, it seemed to work for us, so why fight it.

Speaking of the two of us working so well together . . . I wiggled around on the sofa, making myself even more comfortable, with my head in Brandon's lap and my feet propped up on the far armrest, my bag of chocolates close by, and the journal resting against a convenient pillow. Eggy used his left arm to help steady the book and with his free hand he began to play with my hair. Then, once we were all settled again, we dove back into the mystery of our long-dead lovers, losing track of time as we read about the difficulties of gay life back in the nineteenth century.

"Oh, hey, look!" I pointed out an entry from mid-June to the man who was reading over my shoulder. "This explains why the tunnel didn't just end at the Liberty Hotel . . . '*While the expedient of our secret underground entrance to Beefy's Bagnio has worked quite well so far, I fear that my father is becoming suspicious of the excessive visits I have been making to Andrew's offices. From certain comments he let slip yesterday evening at a social event we were all obligated to attend at the Club, it appears that he is becoming critical of a certain local architect. This negativity raised its head while Father and Uncle were again discussing the proposed Library plans and their search for an architect. I spoke up immediately in favor of Andrew, wherein my father commented that it has already become more than clear just how much I favored Mr. Peebles. And again, later, when I saw Uncle conversing with Andrew's primary rival, Mr. Henry Hobson Richardson, I tried to redirect his attentions towards my own favorite architect, only to be whisked away by Father for yet another lecture. Father was very pointed in his disapproval of how much time I had been spending in Mr. Peebles' company of late, and how many in our social circle had begun whispering about our association. Needless to say, Father was not at all pleased, as he is always so very defensive on the matter of our family's reputation. I fear that I must curtail my future visits to Andrew's abode or risk not only exposing our special kindredship but possibly also harming Andrew's future professional opportunities. However, when I quietly mentioned the same to him later that night, Andrew refused to concede to my warnings. He professed that he can not bear the thought of the two of us parting and insisted that he will somehow find another solution. When I jokingly suggested that he would have to build us yet another tunnel so that I can be NOT seen going to his building so as to NOT be seen going to Beefy's, he actually thought that a brilliant suggestion. At this rate, it seems, Andrew will be forced to build us tunnels all over the city just so we can carry on with our clandestine activities. I do not know how this will end…'"*

"Man, Peebles really must've had it bad for Young Billy," Brandon stated, voicing the exact same thing I'd been thinking. "I mean, come on . . . How many tunnels did this guy think he could get away with building just so nobody would know he was boning the son of one of the City's most prominent leaders?"

"Well, we know he got away with at least one more, since that tunnel that leads from your basement to the Hotel Liberty goes on from there to points unknown," I concluded with a sigh, setting aside the book and twisting around so I was looking directly up at my man. "I think it was romantic the way Peebles was trying to do everything he could to protect Billy. I mean, think of all the effort and expense he went to. Even if those tunnels were basically already started by the City for sewer lines or something, somebody obviously made them much more extensive and much less sewer-like, and that couldn't have been easy. Peebles was obviously willing to move mountains - or at least tunnel through mountains - for his lover. You don't think that's kinda sweet?"

"I think it's kinda foolish," was Brandon's no-nonsense judgment. "Peebles was risking a hell of a lot - his entire career - just for a nice piece of chicken? I hope this Billy kid was worth it."

"Yeah," I sighed, a little put off by my boyfriend's unromantic side. "Makes you wonder though; where does that other arm of the tunnel go to?"

*****

Chapter 4

The Adventure

Despite all my pushing, I couldn't get Eggy to agree to let me go back down into his basement so I could find out where that remaining arm of the tunnel led. He was getting so much better about things lately that I didn't expect such a backlash. But he was adamant that I wasn't going back into that 'damned tunnel' alone no matter how much the mystery of it was killing me.

For the next week or so, though, my life got busy and, for a while at least, even I didn't have time to think about Billy, Peebles, or their tunnels. My new classes were interesting and challenging, but the professors all started heaping on more homework than was physically possible to accomplish in the time given. Sharon was in a bind because one of her waiters quit on her without notice, so she was begging me to take whatever Diner shifts I could fit in between classes. My mother was off on a tangent where she had decided that we needed to do more 'family' stuff together and demanded that I come out to her condo for dinner at least a couple of times a week. And somehow I still had to fit in time to stop in to see Eggy, because I couldn't live without my daily hermit fix. With all that going on, you can see why there wasn't time to read more of Billy's journal, let alone go tunnel exploring.

It wasn't until about a week or so later - after I got a demanding text from Darla ordering me to actually come home that night and spend time with her or else she'd throw all my stuff out on the sidewalk (and she would totally do it, too) - that I had enough downtime to think about what we'd already discovered.

"So, this Billy guy was boning your architect, Peebles, who was so heels-over-head in love with the boy that he put in all these tunnels all over the city so they wouldn't get caught?" Darla summed up the state of things after I showed her the journal and explained the story. "That's kinda romantic," she sighed dreamily as she ran her fingers over the browning pages. "I mean, romantic but completely crazy at the same time," she laughed. "I think I'd call the police if some guy from work did that."

"I know, right? The worst part is, going by some of the stuff Billy was writing, he wasn't nearly as into Peebles as Peebles was into him." I took back the bowl of popcorn that Darla was bogarting and stuffed some in my maw. "I kinda feel bad for Peebles, you know? He seems like a nice guy, even if he was way too old for a kid like Billy, but he really did do everything he could to protect his younger lover. Somehow, though, I don't see it ending well."

"That sucks. I mean, you build like a million miles of tunnels so your lover won't get caught by his overbearing family and then the kid doesn't even appreciate it? That's kinda douchey." Darla popped open the top of a soda can to wash down her last handful of popcorn. "So, does the journal say where the other part of the tunnel goes?"

"No. At least not the parts of the journal I've read so far. I haven't read the whole thing, though. I've been busy."

Darla laughed at my understatement. "No duh! I was beginning to wonder if you even remembered how to get back here." She tossed a kernel of popcorn into my face and giggled at me when I gave her a dirty look. "If I hadn't ordered you back here tonight, your bed might still be unused."

"Probably. But why would I want to sleep here - alone - when I've got a much better bed, one filled with a hot hermit, to sleep in instead," I stated, blushing at my confession.

"Get out!" Darla practically screamed my ear off, slugging me in the shoulder to emphasize just how excited she was. "You and Eggy are actually sleeping together? How did you work that? And what ELSE are you doing together? Huh? Tell me EVERY-THING and leave nothing out."

So I filled her in, because Dar and I had always shared pretty much everything, and this was one thing that I was certainly happy to brag about. She seemed really impressed by how quickly Brandon had progressed considering the extent of his OCD symptoms. I attributed it all to my amazing therapy acumen. Darla said it was more likely due to my amazingly shapely ass. We both ended up giggling away together like loons.

When we finally sobered up, the conversation turned back to more serious matters, like the ongoing mystery underlying my Hermit's building. "So, when are we gonna go find out where that tunnel leads to? If it's not in the journal, we need to investigate personally, right?"

"I would, but Brandon's super freaked out by even the idea of me going back into those tunnels. I mean, he's doing so much better these days, and I don't want to undermine all that goodness by pushing too far. But, yeah, personally I'd love to finish exploring down there. Considering what I found in the basement of the Hotel Liberty, can you imagine what else might be down there?"

"I know, right? It's like looking for buried pirate treasure or something," Dar enthused, an eager glint in her big brown eyes.

"Well, I don't know about any treasure, but I sure as shit want to find the answers to all this mystery," I agreed with her. "You know how much I hate it when I've got some puzzle that I can't quite solve. It eats at me until I figure it out. And this is one huge fucking puzzle."

We sat around talking it all through for the rest of the evening until we ran out of popcorn and soda. The upshot of the conversation was that Darla agreed to pick me up from TAIP after I got out of class the next day so she could accompany me back into Egbert's tunnels. We figured that, with the both of us ganging up on him, Eggy wouldn't be able to resist our pleading and would allow us to continue our adventuring. It had always worked on our parents, so I had high hopes that together we'd wear him down.

"Hey, Eggy! Long time no see, Handsome!" Darla greeted my poor unsuspecting recluse when we showed up en masse at his door the next afternoon.

"Uh, yeah, hi, Darla . . ."

Brandon looked like he was about to bolt for half a second, so I swooped in and distracted him with a nice, long, slow, intense kiss that left us both so breathless and hard that I almost forgot Dar was still standing there.

"Don't mind her, Eggy. Dar just came by to be my wing person and safety monitor while I invade your basement again," I explained when the kissing ended, trying to joke my way through the shitstorm I knew was coming.

"Tristan, I told you, I don't think it's a good idea to be messing around in hundred and thirty year old tunnels . . ."

"I know. I know. But I just can't stand not knowing, Eggy. Besides, the tunnels have held up this long, I don't see why my going down there would cause them to come tumbling down.

Plus, as long as I have Dar with me as my backup, she'll make sure nothing bad happens to me. Right, Dar?"

Darla nodded emphatically, but nothing seemed to dissuade Brandon of his nebulous fears about all the bad things that were going to happen to us if we went back down into the tunnels. Finally, Darla, expeditious as always, just took matters into her own hands, ignored Brandon's ongoing protests, and headed into the old pizza place on her own. Brandon and I trotted after her. When we all came to the locked door that led down to the basement, Dar stood there, pointing authoritatively at the lock and giving Brandon that look like he was a naughty toddler who needed to buck up already. It worked on him just as well as it had always worked on me. In mere seconds, Eggy was obediently unlocking the door and then standing back so that Dar and I could precede him down the narrow stairs.

Brandon was more than a little antsy as I worked the secret door to the hidden room and then pushed the big chest of drawers away so we could open the door to the tunnel. Out of the corner of my eye I could see his fingers nervously twisting at the hem of the t-shirt he was wearing. I felt for him, really, I did, but not enough to stop. Despite my earlier misadventure and sprained ankle, I knew there wasn't any real danger in going into the tunnels again. He was just projecting his fears onto me. There wasn't any way to prove that to him, though, without just doing it. Or at least that's what I thought at the time.

Meanwhile, Darla was rifling through my bag and pulling out the flashlights we'd brought, making sure that they were working and the beams were bright and strong. When the door was opened, she bounced over to me and handed off one of the flashlights. I could tell by the bubbling energy wafting off her that my BFF was just a tiny bit excited by the prospect of our adventure. However, before I could join her in her fervor, I had to take care of my man.

Walking up to Brandon I boldly wrapped my arms around his waist and pulled him close enough for a reassuring kiss. "We'll be fine, Eggy. I promise."

"You can't promise that. You have no fucking idea what's down there," he countered stubbornly.

"You're right. I don't. Oooh, maybe there's a scary monster that's been locked down there since time began," I smiled.

"Tristan, don't fucking patronize me," he sighed loudly and pulled me in tighter, our bodies now pressed firmly together.

"I know. I'm sorry. If it makes you feel any better I'm pretty sure it's just a long, empty, unused tunnel," I replied, losing my battle with my sense of humor and adding, "but if we come across a nest of vampires or a dragon's den, at least I'll have died in an exciting and memorable way, right?"

"Brat!" he complained, with a hint of a smile finally breaking through the mask of worry.

"Now, we're determined to find the end of the tunnel, so it might take a while, okay? I don't want you freaking out if we're not back in ten minutes or anything. But I promise not to dilly dally too much and we'll come right back here as soon as we can." He looked ready to panic again. "You know, you don't have to stay down here and wait for us. You can go back upstairs. Do something productive, or at least distracting, so you're not just standing here, imagining the worst, and coming unglued."

Brandon shook his head. "No. I'm staying down here. I don't think I could concentrate on anything else."

"Fine. Suit yourself, Eggy." I freed myself from his arms and joined Darla at the tunnel entrance. "Okay. Be right back . . ."

We stepped into the murkiness of the long dark tunnel, leaving Eggy standing sentinel in the doorway, and headed off on our mission of discovery. I was well familiar with the first leg of the tunnel so we didn't waste any time, trotting around all the piles of rubble, under the skylights, and then around the first bend. Dar took the lead through the second section, beating me to the door of the Hotel Liberty and then yelling for me to hurry up. I hadn't bothered to lock up after my previous visit, though, so she already had the door opened by the time I caught up to her. We scrambled through the door and I flicked the switch that lit up the big glass light fixtures, illuminating the red-bedecked room.

"Wow! Sweet!" Darla exclaimed as she ran her fingers along the dusty top of the long bar. "This place is legit. I could so see us hanging out here and drinking some night. Too bad the folks upstairs don't even know it exists."

"All the better for us to keep it to ourselves," I replied. "A secret hideaway isn't any fun if it isn't secret."

"True dat!" she agreed with me. "So, show me all the antique dildos!" Darla, straight to the point, as usual.

I obliged, pulling open the cupboard and showing her the drawers, laughing as Dar exclaimed over all the dangerous looking toys she found. While she was doing that, I took a minute or two to examine the side wall, looking for some mechanism that might open up a hidden door to the rest of the building. It took a little bit of searching, but eventually I discovered that the crack between the wall and the panelling that made up the last section of the shelving behind the bar was a larger, darker gap than necessary. Trailing my fingers over the woodwork, I found a piece of decorative scrollwork that, when pressed, seemed to give. I heard a metallic click and then stepped back with a triumphant smile as that whole section of shelving swivelled inward.

"Aha! Found the exit!" I announced to my friend.

Dar joined me and we peeked our heads around the opening, finding nothing more than another small, almost empty, basement room. In the corner I could see some HVAC equipment and there were the usual piles of random junk strewn around, but nothing of real interest. Which was good, because I really didn't want to spend my time here anyway; I wanted to follow that tunnel.

"You seen enough for now?" I asked my companion in crime, and Darla nodded her agreement. "Okay. Let's go find out where our tunnel leads."

We shut the basement door to Beefy's Bar and Dildo Emporium and made sure the drawers and cupboards were all closed as well, then switched off the lights and headed back out. The tunnel took a sharp left turn - more than ninety degrees - just beyond the door that led into the Hotel Liberty, so we headed around this corner and flashed our lights along the next, unknown, stretch of darkness.

This section of the tunnel looked, if anything, more disused than the section closer to Eggy's building. It was darker too. There was only one, exceedingly dim, patch of light at the far end of the passageway, but it wasn't nearly enough to illuminate the space to any reasonable degree. There was also a lot more damage to the walls and ceiling in this section. The piles of loose bricks and assorted rubble made the floor almost unnavigable in spots. At one point there had even been a small cave in on the right side, the crumbled brick and cement exposing a cracked metal pipe that dribbled foul-smelling liquid into a muddy puddle on the floor. I made a mental note NOT to inform Egbert about that little factoid, as it would only serve to strengthen his arguments about the tunnels being unsafe.

Despite all this, though, Dar and I managed to make our way pretty well. When we arrived at the spot where that dim glow trickled down from the ceiling, you could see it was coming from another skylight built into the sidewalk above. When you looked up, however, all you could see was something large and dark blocking out all but a three inch wide strip of the glass blocks. No wonder it was pitch black down here, right?

By whatever dim light the blocked skylight did provide, though, we could see that the tunnel took yet another turn at that point. This corner was an almost perfect ninety degree angle, heading us off to the right again. Unfortunately, by that point I was totally turned around. I quickly pulled my phone out of my pocket and tapped on the compass app icon; according to that, we were now headed roughly south-southwest. That was about all I could tell, though, since I didn't have enough of a signal to make the map app work. Stupid tunnels.

"Should we go on, or turn back?" Darla asked, shining her flashlight ahead of her into the new section of tunnel. "There's absolutely no light down this way at all."

"I'm not going back till we reach the end of this tunnel."

"Okay, then. Lead on, Marco Polo," she teased, stepping aside to let me take point.

This last section of tunnel was in the worst repair of all. We saw at least two more cave-ins and there was a lot more dampness from questionable sources. It kinda stunk, but at least there wasn't any visible sewage or anything. It was just dank and musty and stale smelling. We carefully made our way over and around whatever obstacles we found, including one especially tricky spot where we had to crawl over a large concrete block that stuck out from the left wall, pretty much blocking the entire passage. Luckily, this branch of the tunnel network was the shortest yet, so it didn't take us too long to reach the end.

And, yes, this time it really was the end. Just a few meters past the big concrete block, the tunnel came to a dead end, our progress halted by a rusty metal grate that blocked the entire passageway. The grating had a small gate in it - just big enough for a person to get through, but only if he or she ducked down - which was secured by a very old looking lock. I tried shaking the gate, testing the strength of the lock, but the whole thing was so badly corroded that it barely budged. If anything, the lock apparatus seemed even more rusted than the rest of it, making it doubtful that I could get it open even assuming I could pick such a relic. Looking through the bars of the grating, I could see the tunnel ended just a few meters further on, with steps leading upward, presumably to the surface, except that the exit was blocked with some sort of metal plate. It probably wasn't worth it to even try to get out that way.

However, there appeared to be a second option. Just to the left of the grating leading out of the tunnel, there was a doorway secured by what looked like an ordinary-looking, grey, metal door. This door was even fairly modern, at least compared to the tunnel. It was secured with a standard deadbolt lock; not a problem for Egbert's favorite burglar. The only question was where this doorway led to and would we be immediately arrested for breaking and entering if I picked the lock and we let ourselves out that way.

I looked sideways at Darla, silently questioning her whether we should try the door or just turn around and go back. Dar scrunched up her face, her head tilted to the left as she thought. In the end, all she gave me was a shrug and a 'whatever' gesture, leaving the decision up to me. Which was a bad call, because I'd always been a bit of a trouble maker, not to mention a notoriously bad decision maker, and right at that moment I was thinking, 'why the hell not?'.

So, without further ado, I pulled my pick set out of the back pocket of my jeans and went to work on the door to the unknown.

"Ever the professional," Darla teased as she watched me work my magic.

It turned out to be a slightly higher than average quality lock, so it was a little tricky to pick. It took me probably close to five minutes to figure it out. Darla stood by, holding her flashlight so I could see what I was doing, and trying not to bug me too much by repeatedly asking how it was going. Just before I was about to give up and say 'fuck it', though, the last of the pins dropped into place and I was able to turn the mechanism, releasing the deadbolt. Then, with a nervous look at my burglary buddy, I pushed down on the door handle and slowly pulled the door open.

I stopped as soon as there was a crack big enough to see through. I was surprised that there was already light coming from behind the door - I'd expected to find myself in another practically empty basement - and I worried that there would be someone in there that would catch us and possibly be angry. I really couldn't see much around the edge of the door, however, so I was forced to keep going, come what may. I carefully opened the door wider, all the while waiting for some shout of protest. When nobody came to investigate, though, I took a deep breath, mentally crossed imaginary fingers, and then poked my head all the way through the opening.

What I saw wasn't what I expected. The room behind the metal door looked like any other storage room, only this one was much cleaner and tidier than most. The area was well lit by several long fluorescent ceiling fixtures. The walls were lined with metal shelving, floor to ceiling, and various items of equipment, tools, and plastic storage bins were stacked on the shelves. A few larger items, like a ladder and a metal cart, were lying on the floor, but nothing was noticeably out of place. The shelving on the far wall was jam packed with bankers' boxes, all prominently labeled by year and chronologically arranged with the oldest years on the top left of the leftmost shelf. Thankfully, there didn't appear to be anyone in the room, despite the lights having been left on.

"Where the fuck are we?" Darla whispered nervously as we both stepped into the room and looked around ourselves more thoroughly.

"No idea," I replied as I examined one of those storage boxes more closely. "Someplace with the cleanest basement ever seen by man, it appears."

Darla followed me, just as curious, lifting the lid of one box so she could snoop inside. "Hmm, looks like old newspapers and pictures and stuff." She fished out an old hard-bound book, opened it to a random page, and 'hmmed' again. "Hmm. It's just like our high school yearbook, only for the graduating class of like a hundred years ago." She turned the book around, holding it up so I could see the array of sepia-tinted photos. "These guys all have the same gay hair as your architect, Tristan. You think your Peebles guy is in here?"

I grabbed the book out of her hands and turned it around so I could read the title on the front. 'Duquesne Club Membership Roster - 1928'.

"I doubt it. Peebles was probably dead by 1928. But some of these other guys in here might have known him," I surmised, handing the book back to Dar so she could return it to the box where it had come from. Then I looked in another box, finding similar items of memorabilia, all of which seemed related to my father's social club. "So, I'm going out on a limb here, and I'm gonna say that I think we somehow emerged in the basement of the Duquesne Club."

"I'd say you're right," Dar agreed as she rifled through more documents. "I guess we know where your architect's tunnel came out . . . I mean, I get connecting up with the Hotel so they could get their orgy thing on, but why hook up his building with some drafty old social club?"

"I don't know. Maybe all the founding fathers of Pittsburgh were closet gays?"

"Yeah, that's likely," Dar scoffed at me.

"I suppose that it was the one place where Billy's family wouldn't give him shit for going," I hypothesized as I worked through the mystery in my mind. "It kinda makes sense, right? According to his journal, Billy was here at the Club all the time for meetings and shit. So his father wouldn't have any reason to complain about him coming here. If he just conveniently left after his meeting by way of the basement exit instead of the front door, who would have been the wiser? He could then go to see his lover, Peebles, or go hang with Beefy's queers, or whatever, without getting caught. It's kinda ingenious actually. I just wonder how Peebles managed it without being found out."

I'm about to look into another of the boxes of memorabilia, looking for an answer to that particular quandary, when I hear voices coming from behind me and a door - not the one we came in through from the tunnel - opened to reveal a young man dressed in the Club's typical waiter uniform; black dress pants, a white button down shirt and a dark maroon vest. This guy is about the same age as I am, maybe a little older, but his stockier build makes him look more mature. I vaguely recognize him from my infrequent visits with my father. In fact, he might have been one of the bartenders at the Christmas party. I can tell right away that he recognizes me.

The initial exclamation our waiter was going to throw at some interloper who had invaded the Club was immediately suffocated and, instead, he offered a more deferential warning. "I'm sorry but this area is for employees only, Sir."

"Of course," I pushed the box I'd been rifling through back onto the shelf and turned around to face the waiter. "I was just showing my guest around and we got turned around." It was a bald-faced lie and everyone knew it but since I was the son of a paying Member this guy would never call me on it. "When we saw all these boxes, though, we got curious. Does the Club keep all it's records? How far back do they go?"

"I don't know. You'd have to talk to the Manager about that, Sir," Mr. Deferential replied even as he held the door open in a clear invitation for me and Darla to get the hell out of there. "We need to lock up now, if you don't mind."

There was no helping it. We couldn't just tell this waiter guy off and go back through the tunnels; not unless we wanted to give away the fact that we'd broken in to start with. So Dar and I let Mr. Waiter Guy lead us out of the room through the regular door, which emptied into a dark and narrow hallway. Mr. Waiter stayed right on our tails the whole way, as if to usher us upstairs and make sure that we wouldn't get into more trouble in rooms that we weren't supposed to be in. We all trooped up the stairs and eventually found ourselves on the main floor of the Club in the back hallway next to the rest rooms. Mr. Waiter watched diligently as I escorted Darla the rest of the way out to the lobby, leaving the disapproving waiter standing guard over the basement stairs.

That's when I looked down at the time display on my phone and realized just how long we'd been gone. I imagined that Brandon would be going insane waiting for us. Shit! I grabbed Darla's arm and we started running back towards Brandon's building.

"Can you fucking believe how close we were to getting caught?" She laughed almost gleefully as we pounded along the pavement of Liberty Avenue.

Thank fuck I was still wearing a support bandage on my ankle because without it I probably would have fallen face first into the road as hard as we were running. I shook my head as I continued sprinting; I was now almost desperate to get back to Brandon and reassure him that I was okay. I can only imagine what was going through his mind right then. But shit, we were so lucky we weren't caught as we were coming in through the door. That's all I needed - getting arrested at my father's social club for breaking and entering - Dad would have been livid.

"That was too fucking close, Dar."

I couldn't help but laugh, though. Maybe it was the adrenaline or something, but as I rattled the door to Eggy's building, kicking it open in my best Burglar imitation, I started laughing almost manically. Darla joined in. I don't think either of us knew what we were actually laughing about, but it was obviously a release that we both needed.

We sped through the lobby, heading for the basement stairs. As the door to the pizza place shut loudly behind us, I suddenly heard Brandon thundering up the stairs from the dungeon. Shit, he didn't look happy. In fact, he looked furious. His face was taut and I could hear him breathing loudly as he stood at the entranceway.

Dar and I had immediately stopped laughing as we saw Brandon barrelling towards us, and the atmosphere in the room suddenly felt thick with tension.

"Brandon, I'm sor . . ."

I didn't get to finish my apology as he rushed towards me, almost tackling me to the ground with the impetus as he threw his arms around me.

"You're okay. Thank fuck, you're okay," he kept repeating this in my ear as he hugged me tighter. "I was so fucking worried, Tristan. You were gone so long. What the hell happened? Actually, you know what? I don't want to know."

"I'm fine. We both are. I'm sorry I worried you," I heard myself apologizing into his chest. The sound of his heart beating furiously against my ear made me feel like a complete and utter asshole. "I didn't mean to be gone so long."

"I thought . . . I don't know what I thought, actually. But it wasn't good."

"We're back now and we're fine," Darla piped up.

I'd forgotten for a second that Darla was still standing next to us. But there she was, using her soothing manner to calm Brandon down, and it was working. I could hear his breathing normalize and his heart was no longer threatening to explode from his chest.

"I'm glad you're okay," and I watched as, without a second thought, Brandon reached his hand out to pat Darla's slightly rumpled and dusty shoulder. It was quick, and I don't think he even knew he was doing it, but Darla's eyes widened ever so slightly; something only a best friend would notice. The moment Brandon's eyes were back on me, I could see her giving me a very subtle thumbs up out of the corner of my eye.

Then, just when I thought this moment couldn't get any better, Brandon wrapped his hands around the sides of my face, holding me in place while he stared intently into my eyes. He just stood there, looking at me while one of his thumbs absentmindedly stroked my cheek. I went to say something but he shook his head, silently telling me to keep whatever I was going to say to myself. The next thing I know, he'd bent down and taken my lips in a deep kiss that almost stole my breath away, and he didn't release me until he'd kissed me thoroughly. The thing that really DID take my breath away - this time with an overwhelming burst of pride - was when my favorite germaphobe used one of his big thumbs to wipe away a small smudge of dirt on my cheek.

He didn't even flinch, he just casually wiped the filth off on the leg of his jeans and then turned, his arm around my waist, and led me and Dar back out through the lobby doors and up to his rooms.

*****

Chapter 5

Brave

My Adventure Pal didn't stay long. We gave Brandon the short story about where the tunnel ended up and why we had to come back overland instead of underground. Except for a few terse yet pertinent questions he was quiet while we told our tale. The whole time, though, he had a virtual death grip on my hand, like he was afraid I'd disappear if he let go for even a second. Any other day and I would have teased him rotten about it, but I could sense how much he needed the contact, so I let it go and just enjoyed the feel of his hand holding mine.

Dar had a shift at the hospital that night, so before long she had to book or she would have been late. Even after she was gone, however, Eggy was still pensive. I started thinking that maybe my dusty clothing was squicking him out or something, so I proposed a shower. From the way Brandon jumped at that suggestion, I figured it was the right call.

I led him into the bathroom and started the water running in the shower. Eggy was strangely passive about the whole thing - not his usual controlling self - which was confusing as shit. I was used to the domineering, OCD, micromanager who liked to be in control of everything within his gleaming tower. I mean, shoot me, but there's something really hot about the way he some-times orders me around, even if it's just complaining about the way I left a dirty spoon on the counter. This more laid back ver-sion of my Hermit was a bit confusing.

Even when we got into the shower together, the hot water pelt-ing down and washing away any residual filth left over from my sojourn in the bowels of the City, Brandon was still wary and too quiet. I wondered if my insisting on exploring the tunnel - against his explicit wishes - might have been too much. Was he angry at me? I hadn't thought he was the type to brood about it, but maybe. In the end I decided there was no help for it and I just needed to bite the bullet.

"I'm sorry for freaking you out by going back into those tunnels, Eggy," I finally said, approaching him carefully with the bar of soap held out in front of me as a sort of peace offering. "If it's any consolation, at least we found the end of the tunnel and I won't be obsessing about that part of the mystery any more." Brandon simply shrugged and continued to work the soap into a lather with his hands. "And the good news is that we proved the tun-nels are at least safe, right?"

"For the moment," he conceded. "That's not to say that they're stable long-term. Hell, you hear about old, forgotten, mine shafts collapsing into sink holes all the time around here. All it takes is a heavy rain and one overloaded semi driving over the top of one of those things and the next thing you know you've got a hole
in the road big enough to swallow a VW."

"Maybe, but ..."

"No buts. I don't want you crawling around in those tunnels any-more, Tristan. I just ... I just don't, okay?"

"I'm done for now. I promise." Then I leaned in to give him a soapy kiss to seal that vow.

Somehow, though, our agreement hadn't alleviated the tension completely. Brandon was still pensive and our shower ended up being just that - two men getting clean - without any of the usual playfulness. I had a bad feeling about it all. I didn't like thinking that Eggy was still angry at me about the tunnel thing despite my apology. But what else could I do or say?

As soon as we were both clean, Brandon abruptly shut off the water and got out, leaving me to drip dry on my own. I started wondering if this was his subtle way of telling me to get lost. I climbed out of the shower on my own and started to towel myself off, mentally prepared to just get dressed and get the hell out of there, but when I reached over to retrieve my shirt from the laundry hamper where Brandon had thrown it, he grabbed my wrist and stopped me.

"You're not getting dressed again, are you?" he asked nervously, biting at his bottom lip and looking up at me almost shyly from behind his impossibly long lashes.

I was so confused. "I thought, maybe, you were still pissed off at me or something and I should just leave. I mean..."

"No. No, I don't want you to leave," he interrupted me and then sighed. "Fuck. I fucking suck at this shit . . ." He started pacing around the small confines of his tiny bathroom, making like a caged beast.

Okay, total disconnect here; guess I was getting my signals totally mixed and he hadn't really wanted me to leave. But whatever was getting my man all riled up, it had to be something big. I could tell Eggy's breathing was becoming more rapid and there was a little tic at the corner of his mouth that was spasming, all indications of just how agitated he was getting. Something was really bothering my guy and I needed to figure it out fast. I let the shirt fall back into the hamper and turned to take my tongue-tied hermit in hand.

"Eggy, stop." I grabbed hold of him on his next pass and took both his hands in my own, pulling him around till he was facing me. "I'm not leaving, okay?"

He nodded his head and I could see his body relax a little at those words, but he was still tightly wound.

"Let's go to bed," I suggested. It was barely starting to get dark outside and I wasn't even remotely tired, but I wanted - no, I needed - to have my man as close to me as possible right then. Something wasn't right with him and I wasn't going anywhere until I knew what was wrong.

Brandon gave me a quick, tight-lipped smile and turned before making his way towards the bedroom. I watched him walking away, bare except for the towel wrapped around his waist, and I felt myself staring at the beautiful muscles in his back. Fuck, he was gorgeous. Once we were in the bedroom I watched as he put on a clean pair of boxers. I went to do the same, but as soon as he saw what I was doing he reached over and stopped me.

"Huh?" I could feel my nose scrunch up in confusion, but he just shook his head.

He sat on the bed and scooted back until his back was against the headboard. "Leave them off."

I nodded silently and went to drop my briefs onto the floor, but caught myself in time and laid them on the back of the chair next to the bed. I then turned around and climbed atop the mattress next to him. Why was I so fucking nervous? Something in Brandon had changed but I couldn't figure out what it was; I only knew that he seemed to have come to some decision and afterwards most of that nervous tension I'd been sensing had dissipated.

"Lay down," he ordered.

I did as I was told, keeping my eyes on his the whole time. I could hear him breathing loudly through his nose, something I noticed he did when he was excited. He then turned himself so that he was laying on his side and leaning slightly over me.

"I . . . Damn it. I . . ." He cleared his throat and took a deep breath while he struggled to find his words.

I placed my hand on his bicep and smiled up at him, giving him one of my best toothy grins. He smiled a little in return and then I felt him lean across me and open the drawer on the bedside table. I didn't even think to look at what he was doing, I was too happy having his chest brush across my face and couldn't help myself as I peppered his skin with small, butterfly-soft kisses. Once he'd retrieved whatever he was looking for, he moved away from me slightly.

"What's the matter?" I asked

Brandon then leaned forward and pressed a small kiss against my lips. "Nothing's the matter."

"Okay . . ." It was then that I noticed what he was clutching so tightly in his hand - one of the flavored condoms I'd been using when I blew him - and I raised one questioning eyebrow.

He must have seen my surprise because he shook his head. "Now, don't be getting any wild ideas," he said solemnly "As much as I want to fuck you into the mattress," he groaned softly, "I'm not ready for that yet." It broke my heart hearing how angry he sounded with himself when he said that. If only he could see just how far he had already come; sometimes it seemed he was too busy listening to his doubts to see how much progress he'd made.

"I swear, I wasn't having any such ideas," I said as seriously as I could. "My brain would never allow me such impure thoughts."

He burst out laughing and the tension in the room went down another half a notch.

Once we'd stopped laughing, I could sense his eyes on me and I felt myself shiver.

He then handed me a coffee flavored condom. "Put this on; slip it on your dick."

I did as I was told, my eyes never leaving his. The tension in the room had shot back up, but this time it was comprised of a delicious sexual frisson, not that sick, futile nervousness. Once the condom was on, I waited patiently for my next instruction. I could feel Brandon doing something behind me and suddenly his hand was on my chest and he'd pushed me down against the stack of pillows he'd been arranging. As my back hit the bed, I let out a whoosh of air.

"This time I'm going to suck YOU off, Tristan," Eggy announced, so matter-of-factly, that I almost forgot to inhale again.

Just hearing him say those words caused my dick to stand at attention. I couldn't believe that, after all this time, my cock would finally be where it had always wanted to be; inside Brandon's hot mouth. Fuck, I could feel myself leaking just thinking about it. I watched as he moved down the bed, spreading my legs and situating himself between them, then gently stroking my hips for a few moments as though he was getting himself accustomed to my skin. After another minute or two, he wriggled down the bed so that he could lay at full length, propped up on his arms. He looked up at me from under his lashes, an almost bashful look on his face, and carefully wrapped his hand around my dick. His grip firmed, he gave a few quick pumps to get my cock primed, then he brought his head down and I could feel him breathing me in as he prepared himself.

I'm embarrassed to say that, at that particular moment, I wanted nothing more than to grab my dick in one hand and his head in the other and shove my coffee flavored cock as deep into his mouth as it would go. Of course, I knew I couldn't do that.

We weren't anywhere close to being ready for something like that. I knew I couldn't rush things; I had to wait for Brandon to make the next move. If I was being honest, I probably needed those few seconds to calm myself down as much as Brandon needed the time to work out how he was going to proceed, so it was a good thing I was able to restrain myself. All in good time, right?

"Ready?" I wasn't sure if he was talking to himself or asking me, but I was definitely ready for this moment; I had been since the moment I'd first set eyes on him.

Then came the moment I'd been waiting for; Brandon leaned down and I watched with squinty eyes as he took my sheathed cock into his mouth. FUCK! My whole body was vibrating and I knew if I didn't try and calm down a little, this would be over before it had really started.

The feel of his hair tickling against my hips as he began to bob up and down, alongside the feel of his tongue swirling around the tip of my cock for a few seconds before he swallowed me down completely, was like some kind of sensory overload. Maybe my brain was short circuiting? Not that I cared when it felt so good. So good. I mean, really, really, REALLY good.

Without warning, my hips began to lift off the bed almost of their own volition. I could hear myself making some sort of wild animal noise that I knew I would be embarrassed about later, not that I could help it. The more my hips moved, the more he worked his tongue into my slit. Then he swallowed me deeper and it felt like my entire cock was being massaged by his constricting throat muscles. My eyes fluttered closed and I kept them tightly shut so I could concentrate on the sensations he was evoking. Which is probably why I was so surprised when, out of nowhere, I felt a stinging slap to my thigh. Okay, if I'm being honest, that not-so-gentle love tap turned me on so fucking much I almost shot right then. I was right on the edge and ready to pop, I just needed a little more . . .

Without thinking about what I was doing, I adjusted my legs, reached down, and began playing with my hole, circling it gently with one finger, feeling it pulse and open with the need to be filled, while Brandon continued to suckle at my over-happy dick. Then, suddenly, Brandon stopped moving and my cock slipped out of his mouth with a pop. I groaned loudly at the loss of contact and opened my eyes to see what was wrong. The look on his face was so hot and his eyes were dark and staring, but he wasn't looking at my dick, he was fixated on my wayward finger which had just made entry into my ass. Fuck, I'd probably taken it too far. I started to panic and began to pull my finger out, when I suddenly felt his hand gripping my wrist.

"Shit, Brandon. I'm sorry. I wasn't thinking . . ."

He shook his head and growled like some sort of hungry bear before pushing my finger back into my spasming hole, guiding me like a puppet-master, moving my finger in and out, hard and fast and deep. His eyes never once left my hole. It was as though he was hypnotized by what he was seeing. And, almost like magic, he seemed to know just when I needed more, pulling my hand out slightly, flicking at my middle finger till I'd moved it next to the first, and then watching as I inserted it alongside my index finger. Brandon groaned loudly at the sight but then went back to giving my dick the attention it so desperately craved.

This time, however, he wasn't just sucking me to death, he was simultaneously finger fucking me like I'd never been fingered before. Yes, it was my own finger inside of me, but he was the one controlling every movement and, if I closed my eyes, I could imagine it was him inside of me, pushing and stretching my hole. I felt my orgasm building up quickly, but like the greedy fuck I am, I still needed more. It didn't matter that my cock was hitting the back of his throat, or that he was pushing two fingers in and out of me like his life depended on it, I needed more. Somehow he knew this too, helping by manipulating my hand so I could insert a third finger. His hand was still wrapped tightly around my wrist, and never too near my probing fingers, but I didn't care. I loved that it was him who was controlling the movements and the speed; it gave me a little insight into what he'd be like when the time came for us to fuck for real. Judging by the way he was working my fingers, my ass was going to be sore for days, but I couldn't care less by that point. I was so far gone. So aroused. So fucking turned on by this crazy, unpredictable, amazing man, that I wanted to scream and cry and then maybe just melt into a puddle at his feet.

But I didn't have time for any of that right then because, just thinking about us finally fucking - along with the push and pull of his hand on my fingers and his hot, wet mouth making love to my cock - sent me over the edge in probably the most intense orgasm I had ever had. My ass clenched around my fingers so tightly it almost hurt, and my dick emptied itself into the condom at an impressive rate. And while all this was happening, Brandon continued to play with my dick inside of his mouth until I was completely empty.

"Fuck!" I realized that wasn't the most eloquent thing to say at a time like that, but I couldn't find any other appropriate words.

"You never know . . ." Brandon replied with a mischievous wink as he climbed up the mattress and laid down next to me. "Maybe sooner than you'd think." I offered up a happy, sated smile for my emboldened lover and rolled over so I could snuggle closer into his side. "It looks like those happy pills Darla's friend made me take are working, otherwise I never would have even dreamed of doing . . . that . . ."

He reached over, pulled a wet wipe out of one of the ubiquitous containers that were everywhere in his place, and handed it over to me so I could cleanse my contaminated fingers. Yeah, good sex was never tidy, but it was nice to see that Brandon wasn't freaking out over the fact, and that he was definitely loosening up a bit finally. When my hands were clean, I stripped off the condom and used another wipe to clean off my cock. While I was doing that, I saw Brandon doing the same.

"Hey, when did you glove up?" I asked, noting the full condom he tossed in the nearby trash can.

"While you were busy rolling around and moaning," he informed me, obviously proud of the fact that he'd been the one making me moan. "Can't believe I shot just from giving someone ELSE a fucking blow job, but what the fuck, right?"

"It's those flavored condoms," I teased. "They'll get you every time."

That caused the big guy to laugh. I really loved that fucking laugh, too. It was big and bold and uninhibited and far too rare. My Eggy should definitely laugh way more often. Right then and there I made that my goal for the foreseeable future.

"So, not that I'm complaining or anything, but what brought all this on?" I asked when we were both quiet again.

"No idea. I just . . . I felt like it." He smiled that sweet, little-boy smile that always made my heart feel all melty. "I've been wanting to try that ever since you brought over those damn condoms - which, by the way, taste horrible. Coffee-flavored my ass. Actually, I'm sure my ass tastes better than that thing - but anyway . . ." Egbert fell silent but I could tell he wasn't done talking so for once I didn't immediately pipe up and fill the void with chatter like I normally would have. Eventually he continued, "you and Darla were gone so long. I was really freaking out, you know? I tried yelling down the tunnel, but I guess you were too far away to hear me. At the end, I was even contemplating heading down the fucking tunnel to come find you, if you can imagine that." I gave him an extra big squeeze with the hand that I had draped around his waist, silently conveying how proud I was of him for even thinking about such a bold move. "I don't know if it's those happy pills, or just the fact that you make me want to do all sorts of shit I haven't dared to even think about in almost a decade, but for about five minutes that was my plan. I was going to march right down that fucking tunnel and come to your rescue."

"Awww! Sorry to disappoint you. Next time I'll make sure to get trapped and await my big, brave savior."

Eggy slapped my hip playfully. "Bite your fucking tongue, Brat." We both chuckled quietly together before Brandon got all serious again and added, "how about you just don't go down there again, huh? I'm not really as brave as all that; I'd probably panic once I got ten meters into the tunnel and then we'd have to have someone else come save both of us."

"I think you're braver than you think," I asserted with a happy sigh as we both settled even deeper into the pillows. "But I don't think any future rescues will be necessary. I don't plan to go back into the tunnels at this point. Now that I know where they go, my curiosity is satisfied. Well, mostly. I'd still love to know how Peebles managed to build his tunnel all the way to the Duquesne Club without somebody saying something. And also, what happened between Peebles and Billy."

"You're a fucking romantic twat, you know that right?"

"Of course," I admit. "But that's why you can't resist me. Because you desperately need some romance in your life, Eggy."

The fact that my brave little recluse didn't even try to deny this assertion, spoke louder than all the words in the world.

*****

Chapter 6

Bizarre Love Triangle

"Why is it that every time I see you these days, you've got your head stuck in a book?"

I looked up to see who was giving me shit, only to find my friend, Zeboria, grinning down at me. Now, don't get me wrong, I really liked Zee - he was an incredibly gifted artist and a generally nice guy - but that's not to say I enjoyed being interrupted. I hadn't had a spare moment to myself in what felt like ages, so when I finally had a chance to spend some time reading further in Billy Carnegie's journal, I didn't appreciate this new distraction. When I saw the greasy musician who was tagging along at Zee's heels, I was even less thrilled. It took everything in me not to sigh loudly at seeing that mousy little face staring back at me.

"Hey, Zee. Ian . . ." I sighed and set aside the journal, realizing I had to be pleasant for at least a couple of minutes if I didn't want to alienate my buddy. "What are you up to this afternoon? I thought you were going to spend the rest of the day in the studio working on your assignment for Professor Reading's Expressionism project?"

Zeboria dumped his backpack and art portfolio off on the floor next to my chair and pulled another of the comfortable big black leather armchairs around for himself. The lounge area of the Student Union was reasonably crowded that afternoon, with kids crashed out on every available couch and chair and a few even slouching on the floor in out of the way corners, leaving Ian without any option other than to perch on the arm of Zee's chair.

Not that Ian seemed to object to the seating options; he wrapped one arm around Zee's neck, as if to steady himself, and proceeded to make a show of the way his fingers twirled and tugged on the larger man's short braids. I even caught him looking at me out of the corner of his eye, and the minute he knew I was looking, he very pointedly leaned over to deposit a quick kiss on Zee's cheek. But if Ian thought he'd make me jealous, he was way off base. The only thing I felt as I watched that over-the-top display was pity for poor Zeboria. Zee had no idea who he'd gotten himself mixed up with. But, whatever. I suppose there's somebody for everyone, right?

". . . I just can't get the composition right. I've redone that one section at least five times but it still seems off somehow. I'm about ready to just scrape the canvas and start over from scratch. Either that or put my fist through it." I eventually tuned into my friend's recitation of his woes relative to the project he'd been struggling with all week. "Anyway, when Ian showed up, I figured it was a good excuse to take a break."

"I came over to tell Zee my fabulous news," Ian interjected boastfully. "I've got a new gig coming up in a few weeks; I'm going to be performing at a private party for this really exclusive social club. One of the members saw my Christmas recital and recommended me. These guys want me so bad, they're paying me double what I normally get. It's quite an honor, not to mention a really sweet deal."

"Sounds great, Ian." I unenthusiastically offered him a tight-lipped smile and then immediately turned my attention back to Zee. "So, I was thinking, what if you went with a more muted palette of colors..."

"It's the Duquesne Club," Ian interrupted, apparently not done being the center of attention. "I'm going to be one of the top-billed entertainers at their Annual Founders Day Gala. It's, like, one of the biggest honors possible in a small town like Pittsburgh, you know? The membership there is made up of the wealthiest and classiest elites in all of Pittsburgh. Maybe even in all of Pennsylvania. It's famous for hosting some of the world's most promising up-and-coming talents - I heard that Itzhak Perlman played there when he was just starting out, and Yo Yo Ma too - so I'll be in great company. I mean, you never know, maybe this'll be the perfect stepping stone to a paying career."

I couldn't help it - that stupid, haughty smirk on Ian's face just got to me somehow - so I just had to show up the arrogant little social climber. "Yeah, I'm familiar with the Duquesne Club. My family have been members since my Great Grandfather's time. By the way, the Founders Day Gala is a total snooze fest. Trust me. The median age of the folks attending that event is, like, a hundred and fifty. You'll be lucky if they all have fresh enough batteries in their hearing aids that they can actually hear you playing. But, yeah, congrats anyway, I guess," I commented, secretly enjoying the way Ian visibly deflated as I popped his superiority bubble. Then I turned my attention back to Zee's artistic problem. "So, like I was saying, I'd go with secondary colors and mute them down more. Make it feel hazy, like the way a horizon looks on a hot summer day, all washed out..."

Zeboria and I spent the next ten minutes or so talking art while Ian stewed and fidgeted, clearly annoyed that he was being left out of the conversation. It was kinda fun, annoying him like that, so I dragged out the discussion a little. I know, I'm a total shit, but that's part of my charm, right? Zeboria seemed oblivious about the tension between me and Ian, which I assumed meant that Ian hadn't told his new squeeze about his previous obsession. But, hey, as long as it kept Ian away from me, Zee was welcome to him.

Eventually Ian got bored listening to the two artists talking about stuff that he didn't know anything about and he started wiggling on his perch. I saw the moment when his hand moved from contentedly playing with Zeboria's hair to tapping on the man's shoulder. But when Zee continued to ignore even that - cuz you know that it's virtually impossible to get an artist's attention when one of us is talking about painting, right? - Ian actually stood up and moved so he was standing directly between the two of us, effectively putting a stop to the discussion.

"Hey, Zee, I thought we were going to go get a bite to eat, Hon," Ian suggested.

"Oh, right . . ." Zeboria hooked his arm through the loop of one backpack strap before standing up and also grabbing his portfolio. "Thanks for the tips on my project, Tristan. I think I'll definitely try out a more muted palette. Good call, man. Damn, I want to get back to it right now." But then he looked over at an impatient Ian and shrugged.

"See you around, Zee." I waved goodbye as the two of them sauntered off towards the cafeteria, happy to have my peace and quiet back, then I dove back into the journal I'd been reading.

'September 30, 1885, All Hail the Pittsburgh Gas and Light Company!', the next journal entry I read began, causing me to chuckle at the author's trademark hyperbole. *'The PG&L utility tunnels have finally made it all the way down Sixth Avenue, even unto the steps of the Duquesne Club. And, even more good news, Andrew has been chosen to supervise the completion of some repairs to the Club's building, such repairs encompassing the refurbishment of the kitchens and the shoring up of portions of the ramshackle old basement to accommodate the installation of a new, improved, coal boiler*

system. Andrew assures me that it will be a simple matter, as part of these improvements, to provide the building with an accessible entrance to the PG&L tunnels, which will allow we two to once again resume a more frequent acquaintance . . .'

Well, that explained the tunnel extension going to the Club. Peebles really was quite resourceful using all those utility tunnels for his private needs. No wonder all the intervening journal entries had been so boring; it sounded like the lovebirds had been kept apart all summer by Billy's overbearing family and were only able to reconnect at the end of September once that tunnel was ready to rock. Now that there was no physical restraint on their relationship, I was expecting the Carnegie Chronicles to heat up again. However, as I read on, I was a bit surprised to find only lukewarm comments about Peebles over the next few weeks. That was curious.

I would have read further, but when I finally looked up and noted the time, I realized I was late for History of The Renaissance. I quickly stashed the journal, legged it across the snow-covered breezeway to get to the adjoining Fine Arts Building, and then took the stairs three at a time up to the second floor. Luckily, my professor was still distributing copies of that day's handouts so I hadn't missed any of the lecture. I grabbed a copy of the lecture notes, and a seat, and tried not to pant and gasp too loudly as my heartbeat slowly came back to normal. Even then my head was filled with images of Victorian Era tunnels, not Renaissance palaces, so it was questionable whether the lecture was any use to me at all.

After my history lecture let out, I went directly to the computer lab to put in some work on my Graphic Design project. We were supposed to create business cards for a hypothetical business; surprise, surprise that I'd decided to create a leasing company for the Triangle Building using one of the millions of photos I'd taken of Brandon's Tower to create a stylized depiction of the building as the background for the business card I was designing. I thought it looked great, even if I did say so myself. Maybe, once Eggy's meds fully kicked in, he might be interested in using these cards I was making to lease out parts of his building again? I mean, you never knew, right?

Once I had the card design pretty much done, I packed up my shit and decided to head over to the building itself, just to get in an Egbert fix, cuz you know if I go too long without a hit of my hermit, I get a little crazy. I think Eggy was just as glad to see me as I was to be there, because as soon as I let myself into his office he took the latte I'd brought for him out of my hand without even pausing to contemplate the germs it might be swathed in, set the cup aside, and immediately took possession of my lips in a toe-curling kiss.

"I take it you're happy to see me?" I purred when I was finally allowed to breathe again.

"Nah, I'm just taking a CPR course online and needed someone to practice on," my Eggy snarked in response, albeit without the necessary grouchy undertone that would make it believable.

"Well, I'm happy to serve in that important role. Feel free to 'resuscitate' me as much as needed."

"Oh, I want to do a LOT more than resuscitate you. Trust me," Brandon replied with a lascivious twinkle in his eye that got me wondering about just how fast those happy pills of Darla's worked. "What I'd like to do is bend you like a pretzel and then…"

"Then what?" I asked, breathlessly, more than ready to be pretzeled, provided it would lead in the direction I was hoping.

Brandon laughed, looking sort of amazed at himself and what he'd been saying. "I don't actually know what I'd do with you after that, to be honest. I just … Well … You weren't here to distract me last night, so I was trolling the internet, and I saw this thing, and the guy was a skinny blond, which sorta made me think of you, only his ass wasn't nearly as nice, but I still thought . . . I mean, you are pretty bendy, so . . ." he spluttered to a stop.

"Brandon Kinney. You naughty boy, you! You were watching porn on the internet last night, weren't you!" I teased him.

He snorted loudly. "I'm a horny gay man; what do you think I do when you aren't here to distract me? Watch reruns of 'Leave It To Beaver'? Of course I watch porn. As often as I fucking can," my horny hermit insisted, sending me into a proxysm of laughter.

"Sorry, Brandon. It's just that, I never thought of you like that. Watching porn. I guess . . . I guess I just assumed you'd find that kind of thing sort of icky."

"No. Not at all," he immediately assured me. "I mean, I can't actually DO any of that stuff . . . not now at least . . . but it doesn't mean I don't enjoy watching it. Dreaming about it. Remembering it."

"Remembering?" That comment threw me for a loop. "Does that mean that you've actually done some of the stuff you're seeing on those porn channels?" Brandon looked at me with a 'seriously?' face. "Sorry, I guess I just assumed . . ."

"Assumed what? That I'd always been this ridiculously pathetic?" Brandon scoffed. "I told you before that I wasn't always like this. I'm not some pansy little virgin, Tristan. Back when I was in college - and even before that - I was out there all the time. I'd even started to build up a bit of a reputation as kind of a stud . . ."

"Wow, I . . ."

"Close your mouth, Brat. It's not that hard to believe, is it?"

I shook my head but ended with a semi-doubtful shrug.

"If it wasn't for my head short-circuiting the way it did when

Donal got sick, I would probably still be out there fucking away like my life depended on it."

So, yeah, I hadn't really thought about that possibility at all. It's not that I hadn't imagined Brandon having sex before - in fact, it's something I thought about A LOT - but, that's all it was; a thought. Hearing him talk like this, knowing that at some point THAT had been his reality … Wow, just, wow … Damn, thinking about Brandon, out there fucking random guys, was getting me all hot and bothered. So many thoughts were running through my mind right then, and before I could even stop myself I started asking questions, the filter on my brain having somehow forgotten to kick in.

"What sort of . . ." My voice cracked like an over-excited pubescent boy and I had to stop and clear my throat before continuing. "What sort of things did you get up to? You know, back then?"

Brandon leaned heavily against his desk and folded his arms. I could feel him watching me and when I looked up he had this look of self-satisfied amusement on his face. Like he was enjoying the memories that were flowing through his mind.

"What didn't I do, would probably be an easier question to answer." Brandon chuckled to himself and that little secret smile on his lips was just way too enticing.

"Tell me. I want to know." My voice sounded so raspy, but fuck me, my mouth had gone suddenly dry and was I instantly as hard as a fucking brick.

"I used to love picking guys up off the dance floor and dragging them to the backroom with me …"

Holy shit! Brandon in a backroom . . . My mind was already off, spinning through a hundred different fantasies.

"Then, depending on what mood I was in, I'd either push them down onto their knees and have them suck me off, fucking their mouths until I knew they couldn't take any more, or I'd shove them up against the wall and fuck their brains out until they couldn't remember their own name."

I couldn't hide the fact that I was now rubbing myself through my jeans.

"So you always topped then?" Jesus, I swear I moaned as I asked him.

Brandon chuckled loudly as he watched my hand moving roughly over the large tent in my jeans.

"Always."

"Fuck!" I'd probably describe myself as pretty versatile, although I secretly preferred bottoming, so Brandon coming right out and saying he was a top had to be a fucking sign; it just had to be.

"Does that surprise you?" Brandon asked, as he walked towards me, getting right up in my personal space and then reaching down to replace the hand fumbling at my crotch with his own.

If I thought I was being rough with my dick, pawing at the bulge extending the thick denim of my jeans, it was nothing compared to the way Brandon started to pull and tug at me through the intervening fabric. You wouldn't think somebody could get that heated from just frotting and fondling through their clothing, but yeah. I stood there, completely in his power, as he took over. His teeth were digging into his bottom lip and his breath was blowing in my face as he exhaled heavily with each jerk of his wrist. I could feel myself getting lightheaded the closer I got to coming, almost like I was going to pass out. I remember thinking, 'I swear, if I fucking die before this man has shoved his cock up my ass, I'm going to be so pissed'.

Then Brandon ordered, "come for me, Tristan."

As soon as he said that, I felt my body just completely let go and I came in my pants with a loud grunt. Spurt after spurt of warm jizz filled my briefs and I just kept on coming. It was fucking glorious and embarrassing all at the same time.

"Tristan? You okay, Brat?" I could see Brandon talking to me, but all I could hear was this loud buzzing in my ears.

"Huh?"

Brandon smacked my ass and threw his head back laughing. "Fuck, I still got it. Do you remember your name?"

I shook my head playfully, loving the cocky look that was now plastered all over my hermit's face. The things this man could do to me - and that was before we'd actually had full-on sex - but now that I had it in my head that he was this brutal, domineering top, I just couldn't stop thinking about how much I wanted him. Judging by the persistent distension of the fly of Brandon's jeans, he was probably thinking about the same thing. I sighed, a little too melodramatically probably, but I couldn't help it; he was just so deliciously tempting and yet so out of reach. I felt a bit guilty about always pushing for more from him. I didn't want him to think I wasn't being understanding of his OCD or that he didn't satisfy me - because even without the Full Monty, I was happier with my Eggy than I remembered being with any of my previous boyfriends, by a longshot - and yet I still wanted more. I mean, let's face it, that cock of his was meant to be used, and keeping it hidden away in his pants was, like, a fucking crime. He really should be out there fucking beautiful men every night in the backrooms of the world. Or, at the very least, fucking ME in the bedroom of his tower. He would be so good at it, you know? Seriously, if he could almost make me forget my own name after just a handjob, what the hell would having his nine inch cock shoved up my ass do to me? I could only imagine.

"Come on, you," Brandon was tugging me after him in the direction of his rooms before I'd even had time to drag my thoughts away from my fantasies and back to reality. "You're a messy, dirty little boy. You need a shower. And while we're in there, maybe you can use one of those horrible tasting condoms you bought to take care of this little problem I have . . ."

After that I jogged ahead, leaving him in my wake as I sprinted to the shower so I could get the water started. The mere thought of having that hefty slab of man meat in my mouth again, made me drool. And, if I couldn't have what I really wanted, at least I could have that, right?

*****

Later that evening, lying in Eggy's big, comfortable bed with my head nestled in the crook of his shoulder and my body feeling happily replete after several more rounds of creative sexiness, I found myself once more marvelling at the fact that I'd finally found someone like Brandon. All those years of dating, the weekends spent trolling through bars and clubs, the many, many men I'd flirted with at the Diner, not to mention the hours spent swiping through Grindr, and in the end I found the perfect man when I'd least expected it, hiding away in an empty old building. It just goes to show that you never know when you'll find 'The One'. Or at least the one I thought was 'The One', even if we were still so new and still figuring out how to make it all work.

Of course, that got me thinking again about Billy and Peebles and how they'd found each other, in part, because of this same building. Maybe there was something more to the mystery of the place than just how it came to have hidden rooms and secret tunnels; maybe there was some unknown quality built into the solid brick of its walls that encouraged gay romance? Like a haunting which only brought happiness to lonely gay boys? Okay, and maybe I'm just a silly, romantic fool.

"What are you giggling about now?" Brandon asked, giving my

shoulder a squeeze with the arm wrapped beneath me.

"Just hypothesizing about how your building is a magical love nest for gay boys," I answered him with another laugh.

"You think so, huh?" Brandon smiled sideways at me, his eyes crinkling up so adorably I felt melty inside. "Brat."

"How else do you explain all the gay romance that's happened under this roof in the past?" I replied, reaching for Billy's journal, which I'd left sitting on the nightstand next to the bed. "See, I found the passage about how Peebles managed to build a tunnel to the Duquesne Club so his lover could still secretly join him, here in Peeble's love hideaway."

I pointed out the passage I'd read just that morning and we speculated over the costs Peebles must have had to go to in order to accommodate his Billy. It was clear that Peebles was pretty much head over heels for young William. Lying there in the arms of my lover, I could relate.

However, as we continued to read through the subsequent journal entries, I began to doubt my theory about the building being the birthplace of some ancient, perfect, gay love. The tone of Billy's entries had changed somehow. He still wrote of Peebles frequently, but with less glowing accolades. It seemed their relationship was becoming more routine. Their romance more rote. Less exciting. Less mysterious. I guess that's what happens to most relationships over time, but . . . Well, it left me feeling somehow deflated. Bereft. Like I was the one growing more and more dissatisfied, which wasn't right at all, not when I was lying in the arms of the most wonderful man I'd ever met. It was disconcerting and I read on with a bit of apprehension about where my ideal romance mystery was leading.

"Huh, looks like Billy finally got a bit of a break from his family. Seems like they up and left town for the winter," Brandon commented, pointing out a new entry. "Peebles' tunnels must have fooled Old Thomas, if he relented and left his rebellious son in charge of business back here in the Pitts."

Brandon began to read the passage aloud, "'*November 4, 1885 - Life here in Our Fair City has once again settled down now that Father and Mother have relocated for the season to the more civilized environs of New York City. I am left here in Pittsburgh, put in charge of father's business interests, albeit with my brother, Frank, and father's business manager, Mr. Cruthers, looking over my shoulder at every turn. My days, therefore, are extraordinarily full, yet tedious. However, there is compensation, as my private time is less scrutinized now that Father is temporarily out of the picture. To celebrate, Andrew convinced his partner, Jay, to accompany us on our visit to Beefy's this evening. I must admit that I was glad of this addition as it means I shall no longer be the Novice of the group. It was also pleasant to have another younger person amongst us. I have often felt set apart as the youngest, by far, of the denizens who frequent Beefy's Den of Iniquity. And, although I feel quite experienced now as compared to how naive I was when I began this journal, I am still the youngest of the Hotel Liberty's patrons. So it is quite refreshing to indoctrinate another newcomer who is closer in age and experience level to myself. Jay seemed to enjoy himself exceedingly, once he had accustomed himself to the amusements offered. I look forward to including him more often in the future . . .'*"

"Sounds to me like the boy had his first three-way," Brandon surmised. "And liked it."

"Yeah . . . Oh, Fuck!" I exclaimed, sitting up abruptly when the full import of this entry finally hit me. "Shit! You know what this means, Brandon?" Eggy continued to just lie there, completely oblivious and unimpressed, while I was reeling. "Jay Frick - Peebles' 'straight' business partner - joined Andrew and Billy at Beefy's!" I shouted, still getting no real reaction from my bed mate. "Don't you get it? Jay Frick was secretly gay and he was fooling around with Andrew and Billy . . . You know, Jay, the guy whose wife KILLED HERSELF after her husband VIOLATED

THEIR MARRIAGE BED!"

"Ohhhhhhh!" It was like a lightbulb turned on in my hermit's brain.

"Oh is right! No wonder Alma was so freaked out! She must have discovered her husband was gay and he was not only sleeping around on her, but doing it with other GUYS!"

"Hence the whole, 'Ruination of your Soul' thing," Brandon added while I nodded at him like a bobble-head doll. "Yeah, that makes a lot more sense now. Discovering your hubby was a fag was probably a real shocker to an uptight Victorian Society Matron. Although, I still think offing yourself over it is a little dramatic, don't you?"

So maybe there really was something to my speculation about the building exuding a gay vibe. I mean, if it could turn a married, straight guy like J.H. Frick to the dark side, who knew, right? And, not that I'm opposed to three-ways in principle and all, but you had to feel a little sorry for poor Alma. An affair is one thing, but a homosexual affair, with more than one other partner, would be a lot to forgive. In that case, though, it would seem that the building wasn't just a gay love nest, but the center of a gay love triangle.

"I've got a great marketing idea once you're ready to start leasing your building out again, Brandon," I voiced my conclusion, thinking back on those business cards I'd designed for my Graphic Arts project and already making mental revisions. "But you'll need to change the name of your building first. Cuz this place isn't just a 'Triangle Building', it's a 'Love Triangle Building'."

*****

Chapter 7

Trust

"There you are!"

I jumped halfway out of my chair at the unexpected voice booming out within the relatively small confines of Egbert's small kitchen. Bill The Cat, just as startled as I was, immediately jumped down from the table where he'd been nibbling on a scrap of turkey I'd been feeding him as we shared a midnight snack. Obviously, Bill knew he was in trouble, since he scurried off out of sight as fast as his furry butt could move. I looked up guiltily at my host, cringing at the look of horror on his poor fuzzy face as he contemplated the outrage of a dirty cat ass on his pristine table. Brandon huffed an angry protest, grabbed the bottle of Lysol Spray and a roll of paper towels, and set about disinfecting pretty much everything in sight. For about half a second I thought he might spray me too, out of an abundance of caution, but thankfully he resisted the impulse.

I didn't say anything, just sat there as unobtrusively as I could manage, until the cleaning frenzy tapered off of its own accord. Then I asked, "so, want me to make you a sandwich too?"

"It's . . ." Brandon scowled at the clock on the microwave. "It's three o'clock in the morning, Tristan. No, I don't want a damn sandwich." I couldn't help it, I chuckled a little at his righteous outrage and, after about ninety seconds, his disapproving glare melted. "What the fuck are you doing up this late anyway. Other than contaminating my kitchen and corrupting my cat, that is?"

"I couldn't sleep," I shrugged, holding up the well-thumbed diary I had been pouring over while I noshed. "I couldn't stop thinking about the mess with Billy and his dueling lovers . . . And I was hungry."

"You're always hungry. I swear you have a fucking bottomless stomach," Brandon shook his head at me but since he was smiling I knew he wasn't really angry. "You realize I've had to quadruple my usual food order since you started hanging out here, don't you?"

"I can't help it. I'm still a growing boy."

"Yeah, and it all goes toward padding your already ample ass."

"Which - judging by the way you were pawing at it earlier - you love. So it's all good, right?" I insisted with my brattiest smile.

Brandon didn't bother to deny it, merely pouring himself a glass of Beam and then pulling up another chair beside me so he could look over my shoulder. "And . . . what's our little nympho, Billy, up to now?"

"Well, from what I can tell, he's started on a course of action you'd approve of; he's developing a taste for gay porn!" I explained, and then began to read aloud the entry I'd just come across.

"'Happy Christmas! We here in the The 'Burgh find ourselves comfortable and well this Holiday Season, despite a vicious cold snap and much snow, which has melted just enough to turn the streets into a muddy soup. Because of the inclemency, I only ventured out briefly

yesterday to see to the one imperative business matter that Father insisted must be completed before the New Year. In order to make that expedition less onerous, however, I included a visit to Andrew's office on the way home and was gratified to receive warm Christmas wishes from my favorite architect. Andrew also gave me a most handsome first edition of Jack Saul's 'The Sins of The Cities of The Plain' - a book that I have heard much discussed and am eager to read for myself despite its controversial reputation. I feel this work may be very educational, a sentiment which Andrew echoed . . .'"

I set the journal aside and picked up my phone next, angling the screen so Brandon could see what I had been looking at. "I googled the book he talks about. It's, like, the very first porn novel ever published."

"Nice. I approve," Brandon concluded as he quickly read through the wikipedia summary.

"I thought you would," I smiled at him and then returned to my reading, not liking where I saw the next few entries heading. "Hmm. Sounds like there's trouble in paradise. Listen to this: *'January 2, 1886 - And another New Year has now come and gone whilst I am still dabbling along in the same fashion. Alas, my celebration of Father Time's annual retirement was rather uneventful this year as my Andrew is currently away in Philadelphia - he is meeting with a potential employer about the construction of a new office building - and could not be present for the festivities. However, there is some good news, as Andrew has won the bid for another job here in Pittsburgh and will therefore remain in residence at least through the completion of that project. Although, as that erection will not commence until at least Spring of next year, while the Deacons of the First Lutheran Church finish securing the financing for their new edifice, he is in need of other employment in the interim, hence the trip to Philadelphia. In the meantime, I have invited Jay Frick to accompany me to the theater this weekend so at least I will have some amusement in my life whilst Andrew is away.'"*

"When the cat's away, the mice will play . . . with the next well-hung cat they can find, apparently," Brandon summed up the state of affairs according to young William's journal. "Billy, Billy, Billy . . . So much for all of Andrew's efforts to hide Billy's deviancy with a thousand miles of tunnels. As soon as his rich sugar Daddy goes out of town, the twink steps out on him. Typical."

I couldn't exactly argue with Eggy, as I skimmed through the next few months of journal entries, which included a few doozies...

'January 14, 1886 - Have decided to use Father's opera tickets this evening. Jay Frick will be joining me, without his wife, as poor Alma is indisposed with a touch of the catarrh. I expect that we boys will somehow manage to amuse ourselves nonetheless.'

'February 7, 1886 - Ran into Jay Frick again this evening at the soiree hosted by Mrs. Charles Boyd. The esteemed Mrs. Boyd was staging one of her locally famed 'Tableau Vivant' - this one of 'The Soldier's Widow'. While I was gratified to have been included amongst the cream of Pittsburgh's elite for this special evening, I was even more elated when Mr. Frick and I were able to steal away from the entertainments, leaving his wife in Mrs. Boyd's capable hands, so that 'the boys' could go partake of more manly pastimes. We ended up passing a very pleasant few hours taking brandy and cigars in the basement sanctuary of the Triangle Building. A most congenial experience.'

'March 22, 1886 - I must say that the amusements offered in Pittsburgh, while I'm sure they are most edifying, can become quite dull after a long, cold winter season. I have been to countless musical evenings, theater performances of questionable quality, and more screeching operas than I care to enumerate. I almost wish Father and Mother would return so that they can once more take up the mantle of the Carnegie Family's social standing. It's likely that I am grumbling more than is strictly necessary, missing Andrew's company as I am. The only bright spot in this dreary scene has been my growing

acquaintance with the young Mr. Frick - a highly diverting and eminently charming companion - who has been quite accommodating in making himself available to join me in some of the more mundane of my social obligations. We are becoming fast friends.'

'April 10, 1886 - I can take the smoke and stench of Pittsburgh no longer! While Spring may be a glorious season in the minds of many, to those of us in this infernal city it means only more rain, more soggy shoes, more mud in the streets, and more unbreathable air as the fog and cold keep the smoke of our local industries from clearing properly. I have had one cold after another these many weeks because of the unhealthy atmosphere. Thankfully, my dear friend Jay has offered to take me with him to his country house for the week. Jay's wife, Alma, will be unable to accompany us, as her sister is nearing the end of her confinement and will require her sibling's company, so it will be just us men. I don't care who will be going, so long as I am allowed to get out of The 'Burgh for a time.'

"Sounds like Billy and Jay were spending way too much time together," Brandon voiced exactly what I was thinking.

Then we read the entries that clinched our suspicions: *'April 12, 1886 - I have done something that I fear is irredeemable but I am so far unable to regret my actions . . . What a terrible quandary! Why, oh why, did I think accepting an invitation to go to the country with Jay would be a wise idea? I should have known, based on our past, overly-cordial relations, that it would not be advisable for we two to spend such inordinate periods of time alone together. It is no excuse that I have been missing Andrew while he was away in Philadelphia these many long months. Nor is it any justification that Jay's wife, Alma has been so ill most of the past winter. And yet, all of these circumstances have combined so that, after one too many snifters of brandy, things have now progressed to a point that I fear we are lost . . .'*

'April 20, 1886 - I am now returned from my Idyll in the Country and I am perplexed as to how that leaves things. I dare not write down all

the developments that occurred over the past fortnight, for fear that this journal might one day be discovered and my secrets exposed, but leave it at the fact that I have betrayed both myself and my dear Andrew. What have I done?'

'May 1, 1886 - Despite my best intentions to amend my ways, and my heartfelt determination to avoid all temptations, I can not stay away. It does not help matters at all that Mr. Frick and I run in the exact same social circles and must, of necessity, see each other on an almost daily basis. Once we are in the same room, I find I can't look away. I am drawn to him like a moth to a flame - I know it is a destructive instinct and yet I'm unable to fight it. Whatever shall we do?'

"Damn, Billy. What the fuck did you go and do that for?" I grumbled, angrier on Peebles' behalf than was logical. Somehow, though, I felt personally betrayed. "I think I have to agree with you, Brandon; Billy was a total nympho. And kind of a slut, too, if we're being honest."

"Now, now, Tristan. We shouldn't judge," Brandon cautioned. "Weren't you the one who was commenting earlier that there was too big a difference in their ages and it wasn't going to end well? You shouldn't be surprised to find yourself proved right."

I growled and complained that I didn't WANT to be right this time as I read aloud the final few entries that confirmed our suspicions about Billy's shifting affections.

"'May 5, 1886 - I have just received a note saying that Andrew has returned from Philadelphia and wishes to see me this evening. I have been in a panic since the moment I read this missive. What am I going to say to him? Should I bear my soul and confess or maintain my silence and hide my shame? I desperately wish that there was anyone I could confide in but, alas, men like myself must perforce live our lives in silence or risk destruction. However, I do not know how I can face Andrew after what I have done.'

"'*May 6, 1886 - It is over! I had to tell him. I went to see Andrew, prepared to stifle my qualms and carry on as if nothing had changed, but he immediately sensed that he'd already lost my heart. He called me out and I was forced to confess all my transgressions. Perhaps it is for the best. They say that absence makes the heart grow fonder, but I did not find that result to be true for myself. My former obsession has grown decidedly cold, perhaps killed by the frosts of winter, or maybe just burned out by the warmth that I found this spring while at Jay's country house. But either way, it was there no more upon Andrew's return. I can only hope that sweet Andrew will find some other to amuse him from here on. Meanwhile, I am determined to remember our time together fondly. I have no regrets other than how I mangled the ending of such a fond interlude.*'"

"Well, so much for the promise of true love," Brandon concluded, shoving back his chair and getting to his feet. "True lust wins out again."

"Don't say that," I argued, closing the disappointing journal and trotting after Eggy as he headed out of the kitchen. "Maybe what Billy and Peebles had wasn't true love - I mean, they were kind of a mismatch, age-wise and all - but that doesn't mean that kind of love doesn't exist. It just means Andrew wasn't the right one for Billy."

"You sound like a silly romantic fool, Tristan," Brandon scoffed disdainfully and stomped off without another word.

I followed Eggy into his bedroom, still clutching Billy's journal in my hand as if I might need it as evidence in whatever argument we were about to have, watching as he tossed the robe he'd been wearing aside and climbed back into bed. I could tell by the tense set of his shoulders and the frown wrinkles on his forehead that he was angry, I just didn't know why. Why did he suddenly seem all closed off, like he was excluding me, both emotionally and maybe physically as well? What had I said to so annoy him? He wasn't seriously THAT offended by my prattling on about 'True Love', was he? It almost felt like he was blaming me for the unhappy ending we'd been reading about in Billy's journal.

I approached the bed cautiously, not completely sure if I was still welcome or not. He didn't even look up, though, when I sat gingerly on the far edge of the mattress. I nervously played with a tiny frayed section on the hemming of the duvet while I wracked my brain to come up with something to say; some way to break through the icy barrier that had appeared between us without warning.

"Egbert?" He still didn't look up, just kept staring at his hands which were clenched around a wad of sheets and blankets. "Brandon, please. Talk to me. Did I say something to piss you off? What's wrong?"

"It's nothing."

"Obviously it's something or you wouldn't be pouting like that."

"I'm not pouting!" he replied, crossing his arms over his chest while his pout got even more exaggerated. I wanted nothing more than to kiss it away, but controlled myself. Now wasn't the time.

It was just so ridiculous - the way he was acting like a grouchy four year old who'd been punished for being naughty - that I found myself laughing out loud. Which, of course, only made Brandon more angry and more pouty. I mean, what a huge Drama Queen, right? So I laughed even harder, eventually falling sideways onto the pillows and rocking back and forth, overcome with mirth. Even when Eggy slapped half-heartedly at me with the back of one hand, trying to get me to shut up, I only laughed harder until tears started to leak out of the corners of my eyes. It got so bad I was sorta gasping, having trouble catching my breath as I literally roared with laughter, and rolling around on the edge of the bed, until I rolled just a little too far and fell all the way off the damned mattress. Which stopped the laughter, at least.

"Are you done giggling yourself silly at my expense, Brat?" Brandon asked, peering down at me over the side of the bed.

"I don't know. Are you done throwing your preschool temper tantrum?" I asked, smiling up at him with one last chuckle.

"You're the biggest fucking brat I've ever met; you know that, right?" he growled at me, although I could tell he wasn't quite as upset as he'd been before, having finally succumbed to the infection of my sense of hilarity.

"Me? You should see yourself when you're acting like a pouty four year old, Eggy. It's kind of adorable."

He relented, no longer frowning, just shaking his head at me the way he always does, like he simply doesn't know WHAT to make of me. "Get up off the floor before you freeze to death, you little idiot," he ordered, holding up the edge of the blankets for me so I could slide back into bed with him.

I immediately stripped off the t-shirt and sweats I'd been wearing and climbed in. He was toasty warm. I naturally rolled over so I was snuggled up against his side, in my usual position, my left hand snaking across his waist to pull him even closer. I smiled and let the warmth of his body seep through my skin.

'Shit, even when he's acting like a baby', I thought to myself, 'he's still beautiful. I still want to be with him. I still love him...'

With that thought bouncing crazily around in my brain, I suddenly realized it was true.

I loved him.

I LOVED this amazingly complex and slightly exasperating

man. Whatever we'd had - the initial attraction, the growing affection, the full-blown lust of our early explorations - it had all been leading up to this. I loved him, OCD rituals, hairy face, temper tantrums, and all. This was something I'd never come close to before. Something I'd never felt before. I was fucking in love. This was it for me.

"Damn…" I mumbled, overwhelmed by my private, earth-shattering, epiphany.

While I had been busy, trying to wrap my head around my stunning new discovery, Brandon had finally begun to explain himself, and I eventually tuned in to what he'd been saying. "I . . . I guess . . . It's just that Billy sounds so . . . So ungrateful, you know? Here's Peebles, working his ass off, spending fuck knows how much money in the process, to protect Billy. Building him secret rooms and staircases and tunnels and showing him the ropes of gay life, which couldn't have been easy back then. And the second he's away on business the annoying little twink just forgets about him? That's gratitude for you, huh? It just goes to prove you can't fucking trust anyone."

Which is when it dawned on me just what the problem was here; Brandon was identifying with Peebles. He saw himself as the older man with the twink lover. He had been lonely and unsure of himself until, almost miraculously, he found a lover who returned his affections. But, even when he'd done all he could to prove his love, Peebles was abandoned; exactly the thing that Brandon himself was scared of, and the reason he'd isolated himself in this safe, empty tower for so long.

"You can trust me, Brandon," I stated boldly.

He snorted softly and turned his head, looking off towards the far corner of the room, preventing me from seeing his expression clearly. But I wasn't going to take that. I grabbed hold of his chin and pulled his face around, propping myself up on my right elbow so I could look directly into his eyes.

"You CAN trust me, Brandon," I insisted. "Despite appearances, I'm not some flighty little Twink. I'm not going to just disappear on you one day."

"You say that now, but . . ."

"No buts," I maintained. "I'm serious here. I'm not like Billy. If anything, I'm more like Peebles." He looked skeptical, so I started listing all my arguments, pointing them out by tapping my fingers against his chest, one at a time, as I went. "I'm an artist who is fascinated with architecture. I'm tenacious; I'll go to ridiculous lengths to get what I want. I'm protective, and maybe even a little bit possessive, of what I perceive to be mine. And, while I might have a bit of a romantic streak in me, I'd like to think it's tempered with practicality. Which is why, you see, I'd do whatever it takes to make sure I can be with the man I love."

He seemed inordinately shocked at my little declaration, staring up at me with little wrinkles of confusion outlining his eyes and a puckering at the downturned corners of his lips. But I refused to look away. I would stare down any doubts he might have. I would pelt him with my truth until he finally believed he could trust me not to take his love and then abandon him. I would infuse him with my own, newfound, certainty.

"Do you trust me?" I asked when I started to see the first flicker of credence peek out from under his long, dark auburn lashes. "Tell me, Brandon, do you trust me?"

I waited. It took him a full minute or more to reply. I could see the arguments - both pro and con - flittering behind his eyelids. But I kept staring at him and refusing to back down. Just when it was starting to feel awkward, though, he relented. I could see the moment he accepted what I was promising him; his whole body seemed to relax, the worry lines on his forehead smoothed out, and he let out the breath he'd been subconsciously holding.

"Yeah," he whispered. "I think I actually do."

"Good."

I leaned in so I could kiss him to seal the promise, loving the way his tentative response gradually became surer the longer our lips remained joined. Damn, for somebody who hated germs, it was pretty amazing how well that boy could kiss, you know? But, just when it was starting to get really heated, I felt him pulling away. I tried to follow him, refusing to relinquish his lips for even a second, but he pushed me away with a small chuckle and leaned across the bed towards the tray full of condoms. However, instead of grabbing one of the flavored ones we'd been using lately, he plucked out one of his personal Trojan XL's, leading me to think my Eggy had something special in mind.

"Go on, slip it on my dick," he ordered imperiously, causing little happy shivers of anticipation to gallop up my spine.

I accepted the small foil packet, tore it open and followed directions like a good little boy, rolling the latex disc all the way down the thickness of his throbbing cock. I immediately started stroking him, expecting that to be where all this was headed, with no objection from me, of course, because fuck knows I loved the weighty feel of holding him in my hand. But before I really got going, he stopped me, handing off another condom and pointing to my own dick. Okay, I thought, mutual handjobs. Sweet. This was trending better and better.

I scrambled to suit up as fast as was humanly possible but when I reached for his cock again, he intercepted me, pushing my body away. I was totally confused by that point. I didn't struggle, though, as the steady pressure of his big hand against my chest continued to press me further and further back until I was lying down all the way with my head against the pillows. It wasn't until he began to climb up the bed, straddling my legs, that I finally got an idea where, exactly, Brandon was going with all this.

Was he really going to . . . Holy shit!

Needless to say, I was kinda shocked. I hadn't seen this coming at all. I didn't think he was anywhere close to being ready for THIS . . . Not that I was going to complain, mind you.

"Relax, Brat," he crooned with that sexy, half-hidden smile peeking out of the wilds of his beard. "You told me I could trust you; now you're going to have to return the favor."

Okay, so, I admit I'd tensed up a bit, but it was only the surprise factor. I absolutely trusted him; I tried to relax as he commanded. However, I was almost afraid to breathe, let alone say anything - worried that if I made the wrong move or said too much he'd stop - so actually relaxing was a tough call.

A minute later, and all my relaxation efforts were completely blown away when Brandon moved around so that he could lift my legs up to his shoulders. His motions were measured but intentional. This was something he wanted and he was making a conscious decision to move forward. And I was so there for all of it! Now I was the one holding my breath expectantly.

Without a word, Brandon snicked open the top of the lube and squirted a heavy dollop directly on the sensitive skin around my hole. I gave a small yelp and jumped. This caused my soon-to-be-lover to grin down at me mischievously.

"It's cold," I complained.

"It'll heat up."

I nodded up at him.

"Now, finger yourself for me," Brandon ordered, pulling back so that he was resting on his haunches, watching my every move.

Did I mention how turned on I was by a domineering Eggy? Shit! I immediately spread my legs and dropped my knees onto the mattress. I felt extremely exposed but the horniest I have ever been in my whole entire life.

I could feel him watching me as I started to run my index finger through the lube around my hole. He was right, this definitely had heated up. I looked over and noticed that the lubricant we were using was one of those high end brands that I could never in my wildest dreams afford, the kind which leaves you feeling all hot and tingly.

"Put your finger inside, Tristan. I'm waiting."

Fuck, he was so sexy when he was being all controlling.

I didn't hesitate; I did as he asked and stuck my finger up my ass. Damn, it felt good. I pumped my finger in and out for a while before he told me to add another. I groaned loudly; the feel of my fingers, the heat from the lube, and the knowledge that he was watching me was almost too much.

"That's it, Tristan. Just like that. Spread your fingers a little."

"Mmmm."

"Now add another finger and lift your ass up for me."

"Mmm, Brandon...this...this feels so good."

"Yeah?" He was grinning at me with the biggest fucking smile and I wanted to kiss him so badly. Scratch that, I NEEDED to kiss him.

"Kiss me," I panted heavily as my fingers continued to work their magic.

As soon as I said it, Brandon was leaning down and taking my lips between his, kissing me like he'd never kissed me before. It was intense and romantic and hotter than hell, all at the same time.

Next, he popped open the lube again, this time applying a generous amount to his condom-coated dick. Was this really about to happen? I felt like I was living in a dream. With his OCD and all that entailed, I'd never actually believed we'd get to this point, at least not this soon, although I'd been more than willing to wait. But if I didn't have to, I was fine with that too. More than fine, to be honest. Hell, I was totally, completely, one hundred percent on board with this development. I dug my fingers a little deeper inside my ass, hitting my prostate just right, and moaned. Fuck, yeah, I was more than ready for what I hoped was coming.

Just then, Brandon reached for the wrist of the hand that was still working at my hole and pulled my fingers out - more roughly than I expected - causing me to groan loudly.

"Look at me, Tristan. I need you to keep your eyes open, okay?"

I nodded and watched as he crawled towards me, effortlessly cinching my legs higher over his shoulders, taking his dick in his hand, and giving it a few strokes before he brought it up to my hole. I heard myself exhale loudly as he rubbed himself teasingly against the sensitive skin of my ass. Shit! I probably wasn't half as nervous the night I lost my virginity - but right then? - yeah, I was a needy, expectant mess.

"Are you ready, Tristan? Are you ready to forget your name?"

"Fuck, yes." Hell, by that point I'd have begged if I thought it would hurry this thing along because I didn't think I'd ever wanted anything more in my entire life.

"Good boy," he breathed out. The look on his face was unreal; he looked exactly the same as he always did, except there was something different in his eyes. Confidence, maybe? I don't know, but I liked it.

I locked eyes with Brandon as I felt him begin to slowly push inside of me, but he soon looked away, his eyes focused on his dick, watching in amazement as he slowly entered me.

"Look at us, Tristan. Look at how your body is enveloping me so easily, so eagerly. Your ass was made for me."

I shivered at his words. The feeling of being owned by him at this moment was almost too much - especially when it had all been so unexpected - despite my personal epiphany of a little while earlier. Don't get me wrong, I was perfectly fine being owned by this glorious man, but it was all coming at me so fast. It was a lot to adjust to. I had to take a deep breath and allow myself to relax as he pressed further into me.

Also, did I mention before just how fucking huge Eggy is - my hole was stinging from the stretch even while the fullness inside of me felt amazing - so, yeah, relaxing was a tiny bit problematic here, you know, no matter how much I wanted him.

"More . . . I need all of you," I heard myself begging despite everything and could see myself pawing at his body, trying to pull him closer; proving, once again, that mind over matter was a real thing.

"Shit . . . fuck." Brandon was panting wildly above me as he pushed inside me all the way to his balls.

My body swallowed his cock to the hilt. I was clenching onto it tightly, like I was afraid he might suddenly realize he wasn't ready for this and try to escape. Now that I knew what it felt like to have him inside of me, I couldn't go back. I just couldn't.

"Oh, shit, Brandon . . . Fuck me . . . Harder."

Brandon stopped moving. He looked at me, the lust momentarily clearing from his eyes, and I saw him glance at our connected bodies. For a brief moment I thought that was it, we were done; he was going to freak and pull out. Then he smiled at me, a gloriously happy gleam sparkling in his hazel eyes, and started thrusting his hips like his life depended on it. I swear to all that's gay, he was hitting places inside of me that had never been touched before. I struggled to breath as he relentlessly pushed and pulled, in and out of my body.

"That's it, Tristan. Give yourself to me."

"I am . . . you . . . you have all of me, Brandon. All of me."

I knew I wouldn't last much longer. Not when he was whispering shit like that in my ear and his cock was pumping in and out of my ass, taking me to places I had never been. Plus there was also the whole deliciousness of his weight pressing my body into the mattress. Can you say, Amaaaaaaazing? Fuck, yeah!

When I couldn't take it any longer, I tried to reach for my cock, which was sandwiched between our sweaty bodies, but Brandon kept pushing my hand away.

"Stop it. Don't touch yourself. I want you to come from my cock alone. Are you ready?"

He had the sexiest look in his eyes as he spoke; a mixture of determination and mischief. I nodded my head and, with both hands, I gripped tightly onto his biceps, enjoying the feel of his muscles pulsating under my fingers as he exerted himself. I could feel myself unraveling, the tingling in my spine becoming more and more intense the closer I got to coming. I already knew this orgasm was going to be insane because I was starting to see flashes of lights and I knew I was holding my breath.

"That's it, Tristan. Let go. Come for me."

Well, if he fucking insisted.

It was like I had no control over my body; it was listening to him instead of me. The moment he told me to let go, I did. I felt myself exploding into the condom. I tried to maintain eye contact with the god possessing me, body and soul, but couldn't. My eyes fluttered, eventually squeezing tightly shut, allowing me to enjoy the fireworks going off behind my eyelids as I literally saw stars. I couldn't control how much I was shaking. It was like I'd been caught in the middle of a private electrical storm and the lightning was arcing through my body, sending me into happy convulsions of sensation.

Luckily, the feel of Brandon's powerful orgasm seemed to bring me back a heartbeat later. Somehow it seemed to ground me; it allowed me to once again focus on the reality of this world. I melted back into my bones and savoured the feel of his cock pulsating in my ass.

Finally, Brandon groaned loudly in my ear, collapsing on top of me as he finished.

"Mmhmm," I hummed, enjoying the comforting feeling of the larger body blanketing me. "Not that I'm complaining or anything, but I'm curious. What brought all that on?"

I felt Brandon's weight shift as he rolled sideways, leaning over so he could reach down onto the floor beside the bed, and waving the worn diary he found there in my face.

"What? Andrew and Billy's relationship crashing and burning makes you horny? That's kind of twisted, you know?" I joked.

He used the journal to slap me upside the head lightly. "No, wiseass. What I meant is . . ." He laid the diary down atop my chest and tapped at the cover nervously with his fingers as he worked to come up with the words to explain himself. "I guess it was all that shit with Billy and how you were saying it was all about trust." I could feel the tension this discussion caused him, the unease communicated directly through our sweat-plastered bodies, skin to skin. Finally, he just shrugged and let his hand fall still. "You said I could trust you. That you aren't like Billy. And, I just . . . I knew it was true. I knew I COULD trust you. So . . ."

"So . . ." I repeated, offering him a smile that was so big it felt like my face was going to crack wide open.

Because, yeah. Love. And trust. Yeah.

*****

Because, yeah. Love. And trust. Yeah.

*****

Chapter 8

Uncover

I woke up pinned to the mattress under 150-some-pounds of sweaty, naked, hairy man. My ass was ridiculously sore, but in a good way. I smelled like a cum-drenched gym sock that had been left to marinate in an oven for most of the night. My right arm was numb from having the circulation cut off for fuck knows how long. The left side of my face was scratched and sore due to severe beard-burn. And every time I inhaled, there was this one beard hair, longer than all the rest, that tickled my nose and made me want to sneeze.

Yeah, I'd never been happier in my entire fucking life.

If I hadn't needed to piss like a racehorse, I would have liked nothing better than to stay there, cocooned in a warm nest of blankets and weighted down by my lover's body, forever. Unfortunately, it didn't seem like my Eggy was ready to move. I tried to wiggle a little hoping to wake him gently, but he just snored louder than usual into my right ear and settled down more firmly to sleep.

A minute later those snores were matched with an almost equally loud purring in my left ear from the cat perched on the pillow beside my head. I turned my head slightly and looked into the slitted golden eyes of Mr. William Shakespaw. Maybe I was reading too much into the situation, but I thought that Bill was looking at me a little judgmentally, like he knew Brandon and I had done it, and wasn't sure he approved. It made me feel a bit self-conscious, and if I could have freed my arms to shoo him away I would have. But Bill just blinked at me, as if in greeting, and then reached out with one paw to gently pat at my nose. Of course, this didn't help with my allergies any, and combined with the nasal tickling I'd already received via Eggy's beard, my nose decided it wasn't going to take it anymore.

AAAAACHOOOOO!

At least my sneezing finally woke up my man blanket; Brandon startled and rolled away from the now snotty mess I'd become. If I wasn't afraid it would result in more snot explosions, I'd have had to laugh at Eggy's grossed out look when he discovered the mucus and germ-laden state of his bed companion. He rushed to pull several tissues out of the box on his bed stand and shoved them at me insistently.

"Morning!" I burbled, then honked into the wad of kleenex until I was able to breathe correctly again. "Sorry about that. Didn't mean to wake you but your beard was tickling my nose, Big Guy."

"What do you have against my beard?" he mumbled, finally calming a bit now that there wasn't any snot in sight.

I felt myself lean forward until my face was pressed tightly against Brandon's and rubbed my already sore cheek against his prickly beard. I really did love it. It was so rugged. So manly. Mmm.

"I have nothing against your beard, in fact I think it's incredibly sexy. My skin, however, isn't too fond of being torn to pieces every time it comes into contact with that patch of wiry bristles. I mean, normally it's fine when we're just making out, but last night, when you were devouring me like some wild animal, I thought my face might actually catch fire from all the friction." I laughed at how pathetic I sounded, but shit, it hurt.

"Could you be any more fucking dramatic," Brandon scoffed, rubbing self consciously at his beard as he took in the red marks all over my face. "You're probably allergic to me."

I hit him playfully. "Don't even joke about that." Because seriously, that would be just my luck.

Brandon shrugged and climbed out of bed, walking towards the bathroom, all naked and delicious. If I stayed in bed where I was, I could see him staring at himself in the bathroom mirror, but as much as I wanted to just lay back and ogle him and his naked perfection, I still had to piss something fierce. So I got up and padded after him, jumping slightly as my feet hit the cold tiles. I hopped about for a second until I got used to them, but I finally made it to the toilet to take care of business. When I was done, I looked up and saw him smirking at me in the reflection of the mirror.

"You got ants in your pants this morning or something?" he teased.

"Your place is always so cold."

He turned around and wrapped his arms around me tightly. "There, that better?"

"Mmmm," I hummed.

"How about now?" he asked, rubbing his beard roughly against my face and laughing maniacally like the asshole that he was.

"You're a dick."

"I was going to make a really funny comment about you sucking me off, but we have more important things to do."

I scrunched up my face. "What's more important than sucking you off?" This was a legitimate question, because honestly, I couldn't think of anything I'd rather be doing.

"Usually, nothing, but . . ." I watched as he retrieved something from underneath the sink. "This morning, you're going to help me get rid of this thing," he said, scratching at his beard while he examined his hairy self in the mirror.

"Brandon, I was only kidding." Well, I was mostly kidding.

"It's something I've wanted to do for a while. I just . . . I guess the idea of shaving kinda freaked me out, you know? I've had it for so long. Change is . . . not my strong point, as you might have noticed."

I nodded. I knew change was hard for him, and if this was truly something he wanted to do, then I would help him, but I didn't want him to do it just for me. This HAD to be for him.

"Okay, But only if you're sure." I asked. "And I'm not using that." I pointed to the elector razor in his hands. "It'll clog the blades."

"I know," he rolled his eyes at me like I was an idiot. "This is for later. First you'll need to trim it with those," he explained, pointing to the scissors on the countertop. "Then we can either use this," he grinned, waving the electric razor at me. Or, if you're feeling brave, you could try this." He laughed, handing me the sharpest straight edge razor I had ever seen. Judging by the look on his face, I don't think he was expecting me to pick the blade so quickly.

"I swear, you better not slit my throat with that thing." He was joking, but I could tell there was some anxiety behind his words.

"You trust me? Right?" I asked, bumping our hips together to try and lighten his mood.

He nodded seriously. "In theory, yes..."

"Good, then if you will please follow me, Sir." I grinned and pulled him around so that my back was now against the countertop, hopping up and spreading my legs, then pulling him into the vee of my thighs, before placing a hand towel across my legs.

I held the scissors tightly in one hand as I gathered as much hair as I could in the other. "You ready?"

Brandon took a deep breath and eventually nodded.

So I started. I cut as close to the skin as I could. We both watched as the hair fell onto my lap in large chunks. I heard him gulp loudly.

"You wanna take a peak?"

He shook his head, his eyes refusing to look in the mirror. "No, finish it first."

It didn't take long until I'd finished with the scissors, cropping the entirety of his beard close enough to make shaving feasible. I scooted over slightly, depositing the trimmings into the trashcan and filling the sink up with warm water. I then used a washcloth to wet his face and remove as many stray hairs as possible. Finally, I used some ridiculously expensive shaving foam - no idea why he had that in his bathroom when he'd never shaved before, but whatever - and lathered him up real good, making sure to put a huge dollop on his nose, just because I could, and because I'm a little shit like that.

I scooted closer and raised the blade up to his cheek, but he quickly grabbed my hand.

"You do know how to do this, right?"

"It may take me longer than you to actually grow some facial hair, but I have shaved before, you know!" I was being a smart ass.

"Yeah, but this isn't like a normal razor, this thing is extra sharp. It's not some disposable Gillette safety razor, kid."

I leaned forward and gave him a kiss, getting shaving cream all over my face in the process. "I know. But it'll be okay. My father originally taught me to shave using one of these."

The look on his face was priceless. I don't think he was expecting that.

"He taught you to shave using a regular straight blade? What was wrong with using a normal razor like everyone else?"

"Because my father doesn't like being the same as everyone else. He's a pretentious asshole who believes he's truly better than others. He would never touch some tacky piece of plastic like that to his face."

Brandon ran his hands down my bare arms; his way of saying he understood and that he was sorry I was raised by an asshole. I shook my head - I don't know why doing that helps me clear my mind, but it does - and then offered him a smile.

He returned a grin from behind his lather. "Fine. Let's get this done, then. My ass is getting cold standing here," he said, changing the subject from my father.

"Your ass? I'm the one sitting bare-assed on a marble countertop."

He shivered. "I may have come a long way, but please don't tell me that; I don't wanna know anything about your ass touching something besides my cock."

"I'm sorry," I apologized, giving him one last kiss before bringing the razor up to his right cheek and making the first swipe.

There was something incredibly intimate about that moment, and it wasn't just the fact that we were standing there together naked. It was the way he was trusting me with a sharp blade at his throat. The way we worked together, him tilting his head as I directed or turning to the side so I could get to another spot. The way my hands would feel along his jawline to make sure I hadn't missed any spots. We barely spoke; mostly just one word or two whispered here and there, with a subvocal grunt in reply, yet we were communicating so perfectly that you could almost envision the connection we had. It was beyond physical.

It was all about that new trust we shared.

So I took my time, enjoying the moment, as I patiently scraped at his cheeks and chin, removing a section of stubble and then wiping the blade on my towel, before moving to the next area, slowly excavating the real Brandon Kinney. Unearthing the man who'd been hidden behind the mask he'd made for himself. Uncovering the beauty I knew was underneath with each small patch of skin revealed. Until I'd scraped off the last little dribbles of lather from under his nose and it was done.

When I finally looked at the finished product, I let out a loud gasp at the gorgeous man standing before me.

I used a clean corner of the towel to wipe away any last traces of the shaving cream and dropped it in the sink. Then I just sat there, awed into silence, gazing in wonder at the face of the Greek God I'd just uncovered. Because, fuck me, I'd always thought Eggy was handsome, but I'd had no fucking idea that under his scraggly beard he was this damned GORGEOUS!

"Fuuuuuckkkk!" I muttered, at a loss for words.

"What?" Brandon took a step back, startled by my response. "Is it that bad? Am I that hideous?"

"Hideous? Fuck no! Shit, Egbert, you're . . . I don't know if there are adequate words to describe how utterly beautiful you are," I exclaimed, reaching out to pull him back, closer to me.

The skin that had just been unearthed from behind Eggy's whiskers was at least two shades paler than his normal golden complexion, which is probably why the ensuing blush showed up so well. He tried to look away, embarrassed, but I refused to let him. I took hold of his strong, square jaw and physically forced him to look at me. Forced him to stare directly into my eyes. I wanted him to see the truth of my words in my eyes.

"You are stunning, Brandon. You literally take my breath away. It's practically a crime for you to hide yourself away - behind a beard or behind these walls, it doesn't matter - because a work of art, like you, deserves to be worshiped," I declared with all the sincerity I could infuse into the words.

Okay, so maybe I tend towards the hyperbolic at times. I can't help it that I'm passionate about my art - it's just part of my nature - but I'd never felt this passionate about another person before. I mean, I've had my share of boyfriends, even a few I thought I was in love with, but there had never been anyone who'd inspired me with so much - 'reverence' is the only word that came to mind at that moment - with as much reverence as I felt for the amazing man standing in front of me. He was the epitome of physical perfection and his emotional complexity and inherent vulnerability only added to the attraction. I wanted to bow and kiss his feet. I wanted to wrap him in cotton and keep him safe. I wanted to fucking ravish him and eat him alive.

I also wanted to kiss him.

So that's what I did. I reached up with one hand and pulled his newly shorn face down towards me until I could reach his lips. He didn't kiss me back with full force at first. I think he still wasn't convinced of the truth of my words. But eventually he gave in, his lips responding as I bit and nibbled and sucked at him until he relinquished control. That was when I knew he had finally accepted my assertion that I really did find him to be beautiful - or at the very least he was no longer fighting it.

So I kissed him some more in celebration, my hands stroking at his smooth cheeks and my lips following along to nibble at the fresh skin I found whenever I wandered from his mouth. We were both breathless by the time I finally let up.

"Okay, this is what we're going to do next," I declared, getting up off the counter and moving the both of us around so that Brandon was sitting in my place, making him short enough that I could reach his hair. "I'm going to give your hair a little trim, so it matches your newly spiffy face, and then I'm going to sketch you in all your unhairy handsomeness."

Brandon started to protest that he didn't need a haircut too, but I wasn't listening. I'd already grabbed up the scissors and a comb and started to snip at the too-long tendrils that were obscuring his eyebrows. It didn't take me very long to neaten him up. I left it a little longer on top but went ruthlessly short on the sides and above the collar in the back. Shit, was he ever amazing-looking when it was all done. I swear, he could be a fucking model or something, the way he looks. Which is precisely what I wanted him to be - for me - so I hustled him back into the bedroom and arranged him artistically on the bed and spent the next hour or so drawing my Adonis.

*****

Since it was a Saturday, and we'd been up late the night before, I didn't feel at all guilty when I crawled back into bed to join my newly-shorn Samson, who'd dozed off while I was doing my artistic thing. It was pretty evident, though, that this Samson hadn't lost any of his powers despite losing his hair. In fact, he seemed to have more energy than ever, judging by the enthusiasm he showed when he woke me for yet another fuck after about an hour. I had apparently created a monster. Shit, I wasn't sure my ass was up for this development, but I was definitely going to enjoy it in the meantime.

"Fuuuucckkkk!" Eggy sighed as he came, just managing to pull out and remove the condom before he collapsed beside me on the bed. "Have I mentioned how much I missed that all these years?"

"I think your actions make that pretty clear," I replied, stretching out my legs to try and relieve some of the cramping after having been bent in half like a pretzel for the past twenty-some minutes. "Good thing you didn't completely forget how during your hiatus."

"They say it's like riding a bike; you never forget," he grinned at me like a happy goof.

"I'd rather ride you," I hummed, twisting my body around so I could drape myself over the top of him, reveling in the unrestrained touching, not to mention the fact that Eggy wasn't immediately jumping up to disinfect the both of us.

"Sorry, Brat. The spirit is willing but, for once, I think the body will need a few minutes to recover," Brandon half-apologized. "I forgot how much more . . . strenuous . . . real sex is compared to simply jerking off. You can get off either way, but I haven't had to be quite this athletic in a while."

We both chuckled quietly, thinking back over the athleticism of the past few hours. If I was being honest, I really needed a bit of a break myself. Cuz, I do love to bottom, but it had been a while since I'd been fucked that much in such a short period of time. I figured I was gonna need to ease my way back into the role. Either that, or convince Egbert to switch off every so often so my ass had time to recover between rounds. But, no way was I about to argue with my hermit's suggestion that we give ourselves a bit of a break.

On the other hand, after our impromptu nap, I wasn't the least bit sleepy. So, to keep myself occupied while we snuggled - and, yes, it WAS snuggling even though I hesitated to bring that fact to my touchy lover's attention - I reached once more for

Billy's journal. I guess there was something sorta striking in the contrast between whatever Brandon and I had, and the way our relationship was blossoming, and the destruction of the historical love affair I'd been reading about. Maybe I was just projecting my own happiness, but I really wanted Billy and Andrew to figure it out. To come together despite all the adversities they were fighting and the public sentiment of the time. I WANTED them to have a happy ending. It was almost like, if THEY could work things out, even considering all the strikes against them, then Brandon and I would be sure to end up happy as well. Yeah, I knew that was naive, but it didn't change the fact that I was still rooting for Billy and Andrew, despite reading about their breakup.

So, while we were lazing about, I dove into the journal again, only to have my high hopes dashed almost immediately.

'May 8, 1886 - Things have been moving apace and I am amazed at the outcome of these many bewildering developments. One hopes that writing it down will somehow assist in making sense of it all, although that is a tall order. Yesterday, I found out through a mutual acquaintance, that Andrew and Jay had a serious falling out, no doubt in consequence of my dire revelations. Apparently the two almost came to blows, held back only because of the public venue in which this argument came to pass. Thankfully, according to my source, no names were revealed, so I am not discovered as being the basis of their disagreement. However, it seems that the partnership between the two men may be irredeemably broken. I am devastated to have been the cause of this disaster. It was never my intent to come between two such admirable men. Besides, it is not as if Jay were free to act upon our secret leanings - he is a married man. We can never nurture the tendrils of what bloomed between us this Spring. It would be even more impossible than the already impossible situation I have been attempting to keep secret since I first met Andrew. This entire imbroglio is impossible, to be honest . . .

"Damn. Doesn't look like Billy and Andrew are going to be able to work things out," I announced, and showed Brandon the passage I'd just read.

Brandon took over reading at that point, the next entry confirming my fears. "'*May 10, 1886 - Just returned from a private assignation, after receiving a note from Jay that he needed to see me immediately. I met with him at the Hotel Liberty, for lack of other better accommodations, and was astonished to hear this man, who obviously knows how insurmountable the obstacles before us truly are, importuning me to continue our association. I knew I should deny him, send him on his way back to his wife and societal obligations, but I found I could not. I know we are both mad. There is no possible way we can ever attain that of which we dream. And yet I could not send him off or tell him no. How this may work, I have no idea. I will not - can not - deny myself further, though I be damned for it through all eternity.'*"

Brandon shook his head and tossed the folio back to me in disgust. "If you ask me, Billy really is crazy if he thinks he's better off with Jay. No way is that going to end well. Guys like Jay - rich and from a prominent family - don't leave their wives for their cute twinkie boyfriends," Brandon commented, mirroring my own thoughts.

As we continued reading, it quickly became clear that Brandon was right; poor, naive, overly-trusting Billy, really didn't know what he was getting himself into. Worse yet, it seemed that the dalliance with Jay was doing actual harm to old Peebles. The more I read, the more disgusted I got with Billy's flightiness.

'June 12, 1886 - Jay informed me today that he and Andrew have permanently dissolved their association. Jay has obtained the financial support needed to buy out Andrew's interest in the Triangle Building and will be taking over it's management. Andrew is returning to Philadelphia, for the time being, to finalize his work there. He is not slated to return to Pittsburgh until sometime next year, when he will be starting work on the Lutheran church here. I am saddened

by this development but feel it is perhaps for the best. It was exceedingly difficult seeing him at the Club and other social venues. It is my sincere hope that this time away from all the reminders of our past will heal his soul. And, on a personal level, the development makes it easier for Jay and I to continue to build what we have started.'

"And after all Peebles did for the twat? Ingrate," Brandon proclaimed, not any happier with Billy than I was.

"Yeah . . . I don't know. Maybe it will all work out somehow?" I hoped.

Reading on through the next couple of entries, Billy continued to gush about his plans with the new love interest. "*June 15, 1886 - Father has finally returned to Pittsburgh and will thankfully take up the reins of the many business enterprises he and Uncle Andrew had me managing all last winter. I will gladly give up the tedium of acting as their factotum for the time being. And, with all my resurrected freedom, I will hopefully be able to spend more time with my dear Jay . . .'*"

There followed a series of more mundane entries detailing all the many social engagements that Billy enjoyed over the course of that summer. By my calculations he would have been nineteen; a perfect age to 'sow his wild oats' as my grandmother would have said. Reading between the lines of his prosaic descriptions of the many outings and entertainments he and Jay attended together, it certainly sounded like the boy was sowing as many oats as he possibly could. I was torn between empathizing with him over wanting to experience the most out of life - and enjoying his burgeoning relationship with his new lover in the process - and being disappointed with him for leaving Peebles just so he could sneak around behind the back of Jay's wife. Then I reminded myself I wasn't in a position to judge since I had no reference for what life was like as a gay man in that day and age. Even in the best of circumstances it would have been difficult for two gay men to be together back then, but with a society type like the younger brother of Henry Clay Frick, one of the brightest lights amongst Pittsburgh's Steel Elite, it would have been virtually impossible. Still, it didn't make me feel all warm and happy inside to read about their escapades; not like it had when I was reading about Billy and Andrew. I just had a really bad feeling about the whole situation.

That's when I came across the most shocking entry yet.

"Shit! Listen to this," I warned Brandon before reading the whole passage aloud: "'*August 25, 1886 - Disaster! We are discovered! We had gone to Jay's country estate near Lake Conemaugh earlier in the week so as to escape the heat and stench of summertime Pittsburgh. However, too distracted in our own pursuits, we did not hear the carriage when Alma arrived, intending to join us. Alas, she found us 'in flagrante delicto'. Needless to say, there was an extremely unpleasant scene. Alma proceeded to leave in the very same carriage she had arrived in. We promptly packed up and followed her back to the city. Jay says he has not spoken to his wife in the days since, as she has hidden herself away at her sister's and will not see him. What the outcome of this incident will be, no one can tell.'*"

"Called it!" Brandon crowed. "Like it wasn't inevitable that they'd get caught - the way they were practically flaunting it and all. At least Peebles was trying to protect Billy with his fucking tunnels. Sounds to me like this Jay didn't give a damn."

"I don't know about that; it seems like Jay's in the soup along with Billy," I concluded as I started to read the very next entry: "'*September 6, 1886 - I have not written for several days because I have been too desolate to put into words all that has occurred. I have, myself, yet to comprehend it all - perhaps an impossible task - however I will endeavor to relate herein what has transpired. Following our disastrous trip to the country, Jay and I returned to Pittsburgh on the heels of his wife, who absolutely refused to speak with him. Jay, however, remained hopeful that he would eventually be able to reconcile with Alma once he was allowed to somehow explain. Personally, I*" *was doubtful of this, as I couldn't fathom what possible explanation Jay was likely to give that would alleviate her understandable objections. It was not until the Annual Harvest Festival Dinner at the Club that the two were finally brought face to face. I was watching from the wings, trying to remain unobtrusive, as Jay repeatedly attempted to converse with the woman he'd been married to for so many years. From all appearances, the discussion was not going very well. Alma was reluctant to accord poor Jay any quarter. Jay seemed determined to press the matter, though, and in the end he rather loudly demanded that Alma 'cease her ridiculous display of hysterics and return home'. Mrs. Alma did not seem inclined towards this suggestion and, equally vociferously, told Jay to unhand her. Alas, dear Jay did not heed the warning.'"*

At that point I almost didn't want to continue reading - knowing what I knew was the outcome for Alma - but I was too caught up in the story to quit there, so I continued.

"Shit! This is bad," I read on. "'*So, in front of some fifty or more of Pittsburgh's creme de la creme, Mrs. Alma Frick announced that she did not intend to return to the home or the bed of a Sodomite and advised her husband that, if he desired companionship in the future, he should look to his 'man whore', pointing rather dramatically in my direction. Needless to say, the uproar that surrounded this proclamation was earth shattering. Matters were not ameliorated by the presence of both my parents and Jay's older brother at the event. Jay and I were each taken in hand by our respective families and summarily removed from the environs of the club. I have since been subjected to endless lectures, admonishments and threats, all meant to force me to amend my evil ways. I have not been allowed any contact whatsoever with Jay or any of my other associates. I have been told I will be completely disinherited and left destitute if I dare to have any congress with Jay Frick ever again, and I do not doubt the certainty of this outcome. In the meantime, there is ongoing discussion of my ostracism to New York so that I will be kept away from the 'bad influences' here in The Burgh . . .'"*

"I'm not going to say 'I told you so'," Brandon commented with a sour smile. "But I told you so."

And he calls ME a brat?

"Unfortunately . . ." I then turned the page and read the next, even sadder, entry. "'*September 10, 1886 - Tragedy has stricken! All hope that our discovery and disgrace will blow over is lost. Jay's wife, Alma, has cinched the infamy we will be saddled with forevermore by making us all front page news. Alas, Poor Alma has taken her own life! She was found in her sister's guest room, an empty vial of arsenic on her nightstand, and an accusatory note addressed to Jay in her hand. There is no hope that this scandal can be kept quiet. I am lost . . .*'"

From the way the entry was written, it appeared that there should have been more written there, but the bottom half of the page was stained, as if it had suffered water damage of some kind, and the remainder of the journal entry, along with a good many of the following sheets, were torn out. I flipped forward in the book, but there was nothing more. The rest of the journal was blank.

"No!" I yelled at the inanimate journal. "Damn it!"

"What? What the fuck's wrong?" Eggy demanded, startled by my outburst.

I showed him the torn journal page. "It doesn't say what happened. It just . . . It just fucking ends."

Brandon laughed at my dramatic outpouring of emotion, but I couldn't help it. This was totally unexpected.

"Seriously, Brandon. I need to know what happened next. This is fucking crazy."

"Calm down, Brat, you're talking about them like they're your friends. They're just people in a book. Old, dead people to boot."

I huffed loudly. "They're not though. I mean, yeah, they're people in a book," I waved the diary around as though this would help prove my point even more, "but it's not JUST a book, is it? It's a diary, it's real life - it's THEIR real life. I . . . I kinda feel like I know them after reading this." I sank back into the pillows with a huff of disappointment. "You probably think I'm crazy, huh?"

Brandon leaned back, rested his head against the headboard and sighed loudly. "No, I don't think you're crazy. I guess I feel it a little too, although maybe not to the same extent as you." He winked, teasing me to try and make me smile, which sorta worked, as I felt my mouth turning up a little.

"I guess I just wasn't prepared for something like this to happen."

Brandon looked over my shoulder, his curiosity finally getting the better of him, he scanned the final journal entry and huffed a sigh. "I mean, we kinda knew - there was that letter from Alma with the wedding band - but . . . Shit."

"Right?" I didn't know what else to say, I was still so shocked.

I could tell that Brandon empathized with my feelings from the way he pulled me into his arms again, holding onto me more tightly than before, as we both contemplated the unfinished journal. Despite my frustration over the missing pages, I was reassured by the feeling of Brandon's now-smooth cheek rubbing against my own. The contrast between what we had and the troubles of our historic doubles had never been more stark. But just the knowledge that I'd somehow succeeded with Brandon - I'd persisted and worn down his barriers and eventually uncovered the truth behind the grumpy recluse the rest of the world saw - made me more determined than ever to unearth the rest of Billy's love story. I never could resist a puzzle.

I'd solved the mystery of the Triangle Building, and I wasn't

going to give up till I discovered the resolution to Billy Carnegie's mysterious love triangle story either.

*****

Chapter 9

History

Despite all my finely-honed research skills, I had been unable to find out any more about what happened to Billy or Jay after Alma's death.

I'd spent the rest of Saturday afternoon at the library, going so far as to enlist the Research Librarian's help in digging up something more on the participants of the Triangle Building Love Mystery, but neither of us found much. Billy's entire life history came down to nothing more than that one line in his obituary about him being an avid traveler and 'sportsman' who never married. Jay Frick got a few sundry newspaper mentions over the years for working on his family's business endeavors, but despite all the other members of the Frick clan being prominent in the society news of the era, those sources were mostly silent as to Jay. The Librarian found Jay's obituary, dated January 13, 1911, but that item only vaguely recited Jay's family connections, referred to him as a widower, and attributed his death to an automobile accident. For that matter, there wasn't even much more that my librarian friend could find on Andrew Peebles. Peebles did return to Pittsburgh in 1887 to complete construction on the First Lutheran Church, which was consecrated a year later, but after that there were no further records related to Peebles or any subsequent architectural projects. Peebles died in Atlantic City, New Jersey, in 1919 - presumably as one of the millions of casualties of the flu pandemic that ravaged the country at that time. There was no indication that any of the three had further contact after the events that tore them apart in 1885/1886.

After several hours of digging, it seemed I had exhausted all avenues of research except one. While scanning through some digitized copies of the University of Pittsburgh's archives of Henry Clay Frick's US Steel Business Records, I came across one reference to 'family records' that had been bequeathed to Pittsburgh's Duquesne Club Alumnus Committee. It was a tenuous lead at best, but seeing as it was the only remaining avenue my inquisitive self had, I figured it was worth looking into. If there was any hope at all of uncovering the ending to the saga of Billy and Jay, it might be hidden in those fabled personal records.

Hopes high, I walked the few blocks over from the downtown library to the Club. I was in luck that the guy manning the reception desk recognized me so I didn't have to go through the whole song and dance about being the son of a member, etc. But that's where my luck ended. When I explained how I wanted to look at the Frick records, I was referred to the Club's General Manager. Of course, it being late on a Saturday afternoon, the General Manager wasn't available, but the receptionist did call down one of the assistant managers for me to speak with. This guy, however, wasn't inclined to be helpful at all. Wolford - that was his pretentious name, can you believe it - told me that all the Frick Archives were considered private and I'd be required to get permission from one of the members of the Frick family before I'd be allowed to look at them. All my attempts to cajole Wolford into breaking that rule were rebuffed. He was very obviously NOT gay, and my attempt to flirt with him just made him even more intractible. The asshole wouldn't even tell me who to contact or how to get ahold of them to get the permission I'd need. When I got a little pissy about the stonewalling, Wolford told me I needed to leave, and if I didn't he would be reporting my behavior to my father. Basically, it was a dead end delivered with an insult.

I left the club even more frustrated than before. It was infuriating to think that those records were just sitting there inside the building, and that the answers to my questions about what happened to Billy, Jay and the rest were probably waiting for me in those dusty old papers, but that some snooty, officious little prick was keeping me from them. Needless to say, I wasn't in the best of moods when I returned to my Stylite's Tower a few minutes later. Brandon didn't even need to hear the story as to why there was a storm cloud hovering over my head; he just laughed at me, got up from his desk, closed his laptop, and took me into his arms for a consolatory hug. Before I knew what was happening, he had led me to his bed and was fucking the frustration out of me.

I could really get used to this supportive lover thing.

Afterwards, the angry all burned away by the happy post-sex endorphins, I related my research results to my bedmate. Wisely, Egbert just let me vent for a bit. "... I'm sure I could find what I needed pretty quickly if I could just get in there. I bet the records are kept in that basement storage room full of boxes of historical shit - the one Darla and I found. Maybe I could go back through the tunnels ..."

"No! I don't want you fucking around in those damn tunnels, Tristan!" Brandon insisted immediately. "We don't know that they're safe."

"They've held up this long, I'm sure it's fine ..."

"NO! Damn it, Tristan! I just ... I can't deal with the thought of you down there in the dark with all that rubble having fallen off the walls. If you're right, and nobody's been down there in decades, you can't be sure they're safe. I don't want you going down there again. Especially not alone," Brandon implored, rolling over while he spoke so that he was lying on top of me, pinning me to the mattress with his body and pinning me with his stare at the same time. "Please, Tristan. Promise me you won't go back down there. Please?"

Shit. What was I supposed to say? I couldn't just blow off all his worries without feeling super guilty. And he did have a point - I hadn't even told him about the couple of sections that looked like they'd had minor cave-ins because I worried about how much it would scare him - but even I knew it probably wasn't smart to push my luck by hanging out in one-hundred-plus year old tunnels. Still, I didn't want to give up on solving the Triangle Building Love Mystery, and I knew I wouldn't be able to just forget about it.

"There's got to be some other way you can get into the Club to get those records, right?" Brandon persisted, trying to persuade me to stay out of the tunnels by finding an alternative.

"Maybe," I relented a bit. "If I could just find an excuse for being at the Club, I could maybe find a way to sneak downstairs and take a peek. But short of asking my father to take me with him to the next Pittsburgh Business Alliance cocktail party, I don't know how. And, of course, that would mean I'd have to actually spend some time with my father . . ." I finished with a shudder at that unwholesome prospect.

"Well, we wouldn't want that," Brandon assured me.

Then he grabbed another one of the flavored condoms, squirmed down under the covers, rolled it down my all-of-a-sudden-interested-dick, and did this thing with his tongue that distracted me from thoughts of going anywhere for a long, long time.

*****

After a glorious weekend - spent almost exclusively in my Egbert's bed - I reluctantly dragged myself back to school for classes on Monday morning. It was probably a good thing that I was forced to leave the Triangle Building, though, because both me and my ass were exhausted. It seemed like, not only did my new lover not need any sleep, but he had an almost non-existent refractory period, which meant I had been kept quite busy all weekend. Don't get me wrong, I thoroughly enjoyed myself, but I was going to have to learn to restrain Eggy a bit or he was gonna literally fuck me into an early grave.

So it was understandable that I was walking a little stiffly when I straggled into the cafeteria at lunchtime, right? Was it really necessary for my friends to greet me with a round of uproarious laughter at my expense? Great friends, huh?

"Damn, Taylor, you look like shit warmed over," Peter greeted me as he moved a stack of books aside to make a space for me at the table. "What the hell happened to you last weekend?"

"You mean 'who' happened to him," Zeboria teased. "I know well-fucked when I see it, and mmhmm this boy has been fucked good and proper."

"Ohhhh. Poor baby. Need me to go get you a pillow from the lounge for your ass?" Raphael asked, pretending to care about my tender nether regions by patting at my rear.

"Fuck off," I growled at all of them, plunking my bag down next to the chair and setting my lunch on the table before gingerly - very gingerly - sitting down myself. Why were these fucking chairs so damn hard anyway?

"Usually you're in a better mood after you get laid," Peter commented while shaking his head at me. "What's putting that perpetual look of constipation on your face, my friend??"

"Yeah, well, I've never taken on such a BIG project before," I replied, giving a little waggle of my eyebrows at the word 'big' to make the joke work.

The roar of laughter around me caused several heads at neighboring tables to turn our way.

"Oooo! Do tell, Taylor! How BIG was it?" Raphe asked, leaning in expectantly. "Are we talking jumbo sausage style or was it more like a sad little chipolata?"

"Definitely more of a jumbo sausage!" I replied boastfully. "But it's not just the size, it's the . . . enthusiasm . . . I swear he wouldn't let me out of the damn bed all weekend. I had to practically beg for time off to eat. I can still feel him inside me now," I felt myself blushing slightly, which was totally unlike me, but Brandon brought out this softer side of me.

That comment earned me another round of heckling and teasing as they all took additional potshots. It was all good natured, of course. We always gave each other shit about our love lives. It's what friends do. It had just been a long time since I'd personally had anything good to offer, so they were laying it on thick.

"You're all just jealous because I got some and you didn't," I snarked right back at them all as soon as they ran out of comments. "Shit, when was the last time any of YOU losers actually saw any action?"

"I don't know about the rest of these derps, but I got me some this weekend too," Zee bragged with a superior tilt of his head.

"Yeah, but poking your schlong into that goony little fiddler doesn't count," Raphael replied. He really didn't like Ian. In fact, he disliked him so much he refused to call 'The Fiddler' by his name. "That needy hole's been around so much you could land a 747 in there. Seriously though, Zee, I don't get what you see in the dead ting."

"Hey, Ian's not that bad," Zeboria protested, although not all that strenuously, I noted.

"Not as long as you keep him too busy to talk or play that freaking violin," Peter added equitably. "I swear, one time I let him talk me into listening to him play and I thought for a second he was strangling a cat with his bow."

Zeboria snorted a little laugh despite himself. "Which is why I waited till AFTER I fucked him before I told him that I couldn't possibly go hear him play next Friday," Zee explained with a sly look. "He's been begging me to go with him to this fancy social club he's playing at on Friday - trying to talk up the free food and open bar - but I don't think so."

"Good call! I know you're easy, Zee, but at least you're not THAT easy. It's nice to think it takes more than a skank offering free food to get you into bed," Raphe gave him shit and I laughed along.

But while I was laughing, I was also thinking. I remembered Ian talking about playing at the Duquesne Club's Founders' Day Gala and how I'd made fun of him for wanting to go to such a snooze-fest. But it would make a great excuse to get me into the Club and, with everybody busy listening to the entertainment and rushing around to take care of the inevitable hordes of party-goers, it should be easy enough for me to sneak down to the basement to do my research. The only snag being that I'd have to cozy up to Ian and convince him to take me as his 'date' for the night. Ugh!

Remind me again, how much did I really want to find out the ending to Billy's story?

*****

"How do I look?" Ian asked for about the thousandth time, tugging on his perpetually crooked bow tie and fishing for another compliment.

"You look the same as the last time you asked," I replied, failing at my attempts to rein in my natural snark. Then I reminded myself not to blow my cover as Ian's 'date' for the night. "You look fine, Ian. Don't worry. I'm sure nobody's going to be paying that much attention to how you're dressed anyway. It's your music they care about, right?"

"Right," Ian agreed, smiling at me appreciatively. "Alright. Wish me luck. Here I go!"

Before I could stop him, Ian leaned in and kissed me right on the lips. I was too surprised to do anything so I just stood there acting like a statue. It wasn't till Ian headed for the stage set up at the end of the ballroom, giving a little backward wave in my direction as he went, that I shook myself, wiped the taste of him off my lips, and started to move off in the opposite direction. I might have had to pretend to be Ian's date for the evening in order to get into the Club, but there was no way I was sticking around to listen to him play. My acting skills weren't THAT good. I couldn't stand listening to him without getting physically sick to my stomach, and that would definitely blow everything.

I'd been right, though, that the staff at the Club would be running so ragged doing Gala things that security would be a little lax. Both the Doorman and the Club's Social Secretary were busy greeting guests and checking invitations at the front entrance, with their minions busy showing guests to their tables or helping at the coat check, so the reception desk was empty. I hovered in the hallway for a minute or two, dodging waiters carrying trays full of drinks, until I saw my opening, and then dashed down the hallway leading to the back staircase. Hopefully nobody had seen my escape or, if they had, they'd be too busy to care. I didn't pass anyone between the front lobby and the door to the basement records room, so I figured I was good to go.

I was thrilled to discover that the door to the storage room wasn't locked - that would have significantly slowed me down and if I'd risked picking the lock I might have been caught - allowing me to just duck quietly inside. I switched on the lights and locked the door behind me in the hopes of preventing my discovery. The room looked the same as it had the day Darla and I had broken in through the tunnel door. The tricky part, however, was finding the records I was looking for amid all those racks of boxes.

It took me about five minutes till I found a row of boxes that seemed to correspond to the right decade and another ten minutes of pulling off box tops, rifling through piles of ancient papers and books and ledgers, till I found the Frick records. I'd almost missed them since they were segregated into four modern-looking accordion folio files, which threw me off. Luckily I'd spotted the name 'Frick' on the small self-adhesive label that had been affixed to the front of 'Volume One'. But the minute I opened that first file, I knew I'd hit paydirt.

The files were full of all sorts of personal memorabilia. Frick had kept copious family records. In the first folio there were personal letters, photos, yellowed newspaper clippings, even some old club newsletters, all sorted in chronological order. The second folio had what appeared to be legal documents, deeds of trust, marriage licences and birth and death records. The third and fourth folios had actual journals. Jackpot!

I went back to the first folio, starting with the front slot of the accordion, and discovered that someone had prepared an index of the contents of all four files. Hallelujah! That would make my searches eminently easier. Using that index, I quickly sorted through the dross and found some highly enlightening documents.

First I located several newspaper clippings detailing poor

Alma's demise. They didn't reveal much more than what Billy's journal had already told us, though. The incident where Alma had publicly accused her husband, Jay, of sodomy seemed to have been just as big a scandal as you'd assume. There were mentions of it in three different Pittsburgh papers, along with one smaller mention in a society rag from New York City. Then, a week later, there were new articles detailing the circumstances of poor Alma's death and stirring up the rumors surrounding Jay and *'his alleged partner in debauchery, the young Mr. William C. Carnegie'* The final article I came across ended with a concluding line stating that Jay Frick was expected to relocate to New York following his wife's funeral to take up a position working in his brother's offices there. I snapped pictures of several of these clippings with my phone, so I could read them thoroughly at a later time, and then I moved on.

Next I pulled out a sheaf of what appeared to be handwritten minutes from the meetings of the Duquesne Club Commerce Committee. I scanned through them until I came to several entries dated around the fall of 1886. Aha! This was the good stuff!

I was so excited by what I'd found I just had to tell somebody, so I pulled out my phone again and tapped at the screen till I had Eggy on Facetime with me. "I think I found it, Brandon! See! All our answers!" I crowed, holding up the committee minutes and flapping them in front of the camera.

Brandon laughed at me and my enthusiasm. "I can't see a fucking thing if you're going to wave that shit around like that, Brat." I rolled my eyes at him but I was too excited to really be annoyed by him. "So, what did you find? What happened to your Billy?"

"Just as we suspected; he got sent away!" I pointed to the page of minutes I'd been reading through. "See here. The Commerce Committee here at the club held a special meeting in late October of 1886. It says that Thomas Carnegie, Billy's father, was taken ill in September - right about the time of the uproar over

Billy being involved in Alma Frick's death - and had finally succumbed to his illness as of October 19th. The minutes note that Billy would not be able to assume his father's position because he had been sent away to *'scout potential business opportunities in the Western Territories'.*"

"Damn! That sucks for old Thomas. What a drama queen though; he'd rather die than acknowledge his son was a fag? Whatever," Brandon came to the same conclusion I had. "Personally, though, I think Billy got off with a pretty good deal. He got to escape the family and head out west where he was allowed to do his whole 'Sportsman and Traveller' thing. I'm sure he was happier out there than being under the disapproving eyes of his family."

"Yeah, but it explains why nothing more was heard about him. If he was shipped off to the wilds of the 'Western Territories' back in 1886, it's not surprising that he never turned up in any of the social listings in Pittsburgh or New York," I concluded as I continued to read through the rest of the Committee minutes. "Oh, hey, here's a note about Peebles too . . . *'Mr. Andrew Carnegie motioned that the contract formerly extended to Mr. Andrew Peebles for construction of the new Clubhouse be discontinued, citing the architect's abject moral turpitude and Mr. Peebles' involvement in the late unpleasantness associated with the death of Mrs. Alma Frick. The motion was seconded by Mr. Brock-Hampton. After discussion, the matter was put to a vote and the motion carried unanimously.'"*

"Poor S.O.B. They fucking blackballed him," Brandon surmised. "No wonder Peebles didn't get any more work in Pittsburgh. What happened to Alma wasn't even his fault; if Billy hadn't fucked Andrew over for a fling with Jay, they all would have been fine. Still closeted, but fine."

"Yeah, I agree. It totally sucks for Peebles," I concurred, finishing with the Committee Meeting notes and putting them back in the file. "Basically, everyone involved was fucked over. Did I ever mention how fucking happy I am not to have lived back then? Shit, it's hard enough being gay nowadays. I can't even imagine dealing with the crap these guys had to go through."

Eggy agreed with me. We continued to chat about the harsh treatment the 1886 boys had suffered as I sifted through more of the records. I found a few more tidbits here and there, mostly dealing with Jay's work in the New York Offices of H.C. Frick & Company, and later, once the two families had formally merged their businesses, for the Carnegie Steel Company.

I'd just begun to dig through some personal correspondence I found in the back of the file, when I came across one more brief mention of Jay. It was a letter to Henry Clay from none other than Andrew Carnegie dated August, 1892. I skipped over most of the parts that dealt with business stuff - including a lengthy discussion of something called the 'Homestead Strike' - finding a more personal discussion at the conclusion of the letter.

"Listen to this," I announced and read the rest of the passage aloud to Brandon. "*I am disappointed and dismayed at your handling of this matter, Frick. I know we've had our share of difficulties over the years, but we have always managed to put on a united front. Even with that business with your Mary Ann brother and my nephew, which was messy as hell, we were able to work together to quash the ensuing scandal for our two families and have since managed to keep the little catamites separated. However, I can not condone your reckless practices with regard to our current business interests. If you are incapable of handling matters better, I will have you banished along with your degenerate brother to the bowels of the New York office . . .*"

I hadn't had time to finish reading the passage before I heard voices out in the corridor and then someone began to rattle at the doorknob. I looked at the clock on my phone and realized I'd been down here far longer than I'd planned. Shit. I hastily began to stuff the documents I'd pulled out back into the file, intending to try and hide my mischief as best as I could, but hadn't managed to clean it all up when the door to the storage room literally crashed open.

I turned to look and discovered that whoever wanted in hadn't bothered to find a key to the door; they'd apparently just kicked it in, as evidenced by the splintering and cracking of the wood around the door jamb. But the force with which the door had been rammed had backfired and the door had immediately swung closed again after it crashed into the wall behind. Which gave me just enough time to spin around so I was looking at the entryway face-on when the invaders came all the way in.

"There you are! What the hell are you doing down here, skulking in the damn basement?" a drunken and visibly angry Craig Taylor screamed at me.

*****

Chapter 10

When The Deed Is Done

"Dad? What the hell . . ." My father was the absolute LAST person I had expected to see.

"You think you can just come to MY Club and embarrass me by showing off all your faggy ways and get away with it?" Craig continued to rant, not even really acknowledging my question. He pointed over his shoulder with the hand holding his highball glass and, in the process, sloshed the liquor all over himself, but he was apparently too drunk to care. Behind my father I could just barely see the ashen face of my 'date' for the night, Ian. "I saw you, you know," he slurred. "I SAW what you did! You're disgusting. Kissing this other fucking pansy here. And, what's even worse, all my friends and business associates saw you too, damn it! Do you KNOW how fucking humiliating that is? It's bad enough I have to live with the fact that my son is a damned butt-hole ranger, but now you're going to flaunt your sexual deviancy in the faces of all my friends? Fuck you, Tristan! FUCK you!"

Okay, so Dad was more than three sheets to the wind and on a total tear. Not that this was a new experience for me; I grew up dealing with his random drunken nights where he would come home from the Club and talk to my mom like a piece of shit. But this was definitely not something I wanted to deal with right then. Especially not with Ian looking on.

"Dad, I think you've had a little too much to drink. We should probably get you home," I said in my best calming voice. "You're going to regret breaking that door when you get the bill from the Club in the morning, you know."

"Fuck that! And don't you dare try to 'manage' me, you fucking little fairy. If anyone needs to leave this Club it's YOU! We don't need your type around here. Take your little fuck buddy and get the hell out of MY Club before anyone else sees you and realizes I'm related to such trash!"

Yeah. So much for trying to reason with my drunken, homophobic, asshole of a father, right? I mean, a guy can only take so much. I'd known how much he hated my being gay from the moment I came out to him and mom, so the slurs against my sexuality were kinda expected. What I couldn't take was the nastiness with which they were being delivered. Or the way he was basically trying to force me to hide myself and hide the fact that I was gay. I wasn't going back into the closet for an ignorant bigot like Craig Taylor - especially not so he could save his reputation with his equally bigotted buddies. So, despite my best intentions of trying to help Craig get out of the Club without any more of an uproar, I kinda lost it at that point.

"You know what? Fuck YOU, Craig!" I yelled back at him, stepping forward to get right in his face. "I couldn't care less if you or your snobbish friends are offended by my kissing another guy. It's the 21st Century for fuck sake; get over your neanderthal prejudices already! I'm GAY, Craig! YOUR SON IS GAY! And I'll always BE gay, so hiding me from your friends isn't going to help. Hell, if anyone is an embarrassment here, it's you, prancing around here, drunk out of your fucking mind, breaking down doors and screaming out your bigoted bullshit!"

I stood there, chest to chest with the sad, old, bastard that was my father, and stared him defiantly in the eye. I was so done taking his shit. I was done with hiding myself so HE wouldn't be embarrassed by me. I was tired of him being the embarrassment. And I was done listening passively to his constant denigration. For the moment, I'd even forgotten that he still held the purse strings to my education trust fund. I was just so sick and tired of dealing with his prejudices and I wasn't backing down again.

Unfortunately, I'd also sorta forgotten just what a bad idea it was to have a face-off with an irrational drunk.

Craig returned my stare for about thirty seconds, getting redder in the face the entire time, that vein in his left temple enlarging and throbbing, faster and faster as his temper took over. He was literally snorting with anger, his breathing becoming more rapid but having no outlet other than his widely flaring nostrils since his mouth was puckered up in an ugly frown. Out of nowhere, the image of an angry cartoon bull popped into my head and I snickered at the comparison.

I realized a second later that my laughing was probably a mistake.

My little huff of laughter was the last straw for Craig. He furiously smashed his now almost empty whisky glass to the concrete floor, causing shards of glass to fly everywhere. Then Craig lunged at me, wrapping both his newly freed hands around my throat so he could shake me and strangle me at the same time. I tried to pry his fingers away but I was no match for his insane and drunken strength. Worse still, as he was shaking me, the impetus of his movement carried us both along until my back was up against a section of the shelving, and each subsequent shake he delivered caused my head to crack painfully against the rough metal edge behind me. I tried to fight him off but I wasn't very effective; he had sixty pounds on me and his righteous fury gave him the advantage. My few efforts to punch or kick him in an attempt to defend myself only seemed to make Craig more angry. As my oxygen levels began to dwindle, I focused on the face I could still see standing in the doorway beyond Craig's shoulder, but Ian seemed frozen in place and either unable or unwilling to help me.

I don't know how long the struggle with Craig lasted. It felt like it went on forever. It could have been only a few minutes, or it could have been hours. Time ceased to make any sense as he shook me and knocked my body against the shelving while slowly choking me. I fought back as best I could, ineffectually hitting him or kicking at his shins. Nothing seemed to penetrate the violent madness I saw stabbing out at me from the once familiar eyes of the man who was supposed to be my father. Meanwhile, the pain in my head was making me dizzy. My sense of hearing had become disconnected and all the sounds around me felt distant and delayed, causing me even more confusion. Then the lights of the storage room began to dim and my vision tunneled so that I could no longer see anything outside the fisheye lens version of my father's looming face as he attempted to kill me for the sin of being gay.

Just when I was about to pass out completely, I saw this blur of motion coming up from my left. Suddenly Craig was gone and there was nothing holding me up, so I began to collapse towards the floor. Something, or rather someone, caught me just before I hit the cold, hard concrete. I felt two strong arms hoisting me back up to my feet as I gasped for air like a fish out of water. I clung to the tall, sturdy body wrapping itself around me. All I could do was breathe and try not to fall completely apart as I dazedly held fast to the only support I had.

My vision was still sort of wonky, and what I could see was clouded by the tears that had sprung up unwanted, so I wasn't entirely sure what came next. It seemed like everything was happening at once. My hearing returned just as a roar of rage erupted from somewhere on my right. The next thing I knew, whoever had been holding me up was gone. I teetered on my unsteady legs, eventually sliding down the wall of shelving behind me till I was slumped in a heap on the floor.

Meanwhile, in front of me, my father and Brandon were duking it out in what looked like an all-out death match. Ian The Impotent had scooted around the combatants, who were taking up much of the middle of the room, to come to my side; I tried to bat away his overly-solicitous pawing but it felt like I was fighting off an octopus. To make the chaos even more perfect, right at that moment our tiny room was unexpectedly filled with what felt like about a hundred maroon-vested Club staffers, all of whom were shouting and bumbling around doing fuck all, but mostly getting in the way.

When one of the Club guys came over and started groping at me along with Ian, I figured I'd had enough. I punched someone - not sure who, but I think it was maybe Ian judging by his later reaction - and freed myself from the concerned caregivers trying to hold me down. It took a bit of effort, but I managed to struggle to my feet, only to find that the staffers had already pulled Brandon and my dad apart and were holding them on separate sides of the room. A quick scan of both of them reassured me that my father had clearly got the worst of the fight; he was slumped on a pile of boxes, blood dripping down onto his dress shirt from a large gash over his left eye and the corner of his mouth was torn and swollen. Brandon, on the other hand, was still on his feet, still struggling to free himself from those attempting to hold him back, and the only visible blood on him was that decorating his clenched fists.

I waded through the sea of officious do-gooders to get to Brandon. He didn't seem to see me at first, he was so focused on his foe across the room, but that didn't stop me from wrapping my arms around his waist and just holding on for dear life. Eventually, my presence seemed to penetrate the fog of fury surrounding him. I saw him blink and shake his head a little, as if trying to clear away the confusion, then he looked down at me and smiled as if nothing else around us mattered. I beamed my best sunshine grin back at him and my Eggy gently returned my embrace. For that one moment of peace, it was like we were all alone in that tiny room and none of the surrounding pandemonium could touch us. It was too good to last though.

"Tristan. Tristan! Talk to me. Are you okay?" The annoying twang of Ian's voice as he continued to pull at my arms finally broke through the bliss of my reunion with Egbert. "Shit! I thought your dad was going to kill you. When he came over and asked me where you were, I never thought he'd try and kill you. I just thought . . . I didn't know why you'd snuck off without me and I was kinda pissed at you for missing my performance, but I swear I didn't know he'd go batshit crazy like this when I told him which way you'd gone. He just blew up at me . . . I'm so sorry, Tristan . . . Fuck, you're still bleeding. You need to come sit down. We should call a doctor to check you out . . ."

Brandon had distractedly resisted all of Ian's attempts to get me away from him but the mention of me bleeding seemed to finally wake him up. I thought at first he would recoil, what with the whole OCD germaphobe thing, but no. Instead, Brandon's hand came up to the back of my head, tenderly examining with his fingers to see how bad the cuts to my scalp were, and then pulling his bloodied hand away with a renewed glint of anger. But, rather than relinquish me to the importunate Ian, Brandon bent down, scooped me up into his arms and turned as if to head out the gaping door leading out into the tunnels.

"Where the fuck do you think you're going with my son!" Craig bellowed, lurching up off his pile of boxes and moving so as to block Brandon's escape. I was impressed with the fact that he was even able to still function considering how beat up he was, not to mention that his drunk had only got drunker. "I don't know who the fuck you think you are, Buddy, but you're not taking my faggot son anywhere until I get some answers." Craig turned his attention down on me with that familiar disdainful sneer. "You never answered me, Tristan. I asked what the hell you were doing down here. The Club staff told me you were asking around last week about rifling through these records, but they told you to get lost. So what? Now you're sneaking around without permission anyway? That's just like you; a spoiled brat. You always were a fucking disappointment, and not just because you're a pathetic little fairy who can't stand up for himself. I see you found yourself a defender though. Should have known . . . What with you flaunting your ass and making goo-goo eyes at every queer in the City . . . Embarrassing me all over again, just like you did at the damned Christmas party . . . Figures you'd eventually find an even bigger fag than yourself to fight your battles for you."

Okay, still bleeding and shaky after having been practically killed, or not, I wasn't putting up with any more shit from the likes of Craig Taylor.

"Put me down, Brandon," I directed, and he reluctantly obeyed, but remained standing like a bulwark at my back, holding me up and supporting me with his hulking presence. Which gave me the confidence to stand up to Craig again. "Fuck. You. Craig! You don't get to tell me I'm the one in the wrong after you just attempted to murder your own son. What I'm doing and who I do it with are no longer any of your fucking business. I'm through with you. And, for the last time, I'm gay - that's NOT going to change no matter how much you claim it embarrasses you - so get over yourself already, you fucking troglodyte!"

I started to turn away from him, now that I'd had my say, but apparently he wasn't through with me. "Not so fast, boy!" Craig grabbed my shoulder and wrenched me around till I was facing him again. "You don't get to disrespect me like that and then just walk away. I'm still the head of this family and you'll either do as I say - which includes not shaming the Taylor name with your disgusting, perverted lifestyle - or I'll cut you off completely. I'll disinherit you and then you can say goodbye to your fairy art school and your mooching faggot friends and everything else MY money buys you. What do you say to that, you fucking pansy?"

And there it was. The ultimate WASP threat. Do what I say - behave the way I dictate - or I'll take away the money. I'm sure that was pretty much the same argument the Carnegie family used on poor Billy when they sent him off to the wilds of the Western Territories all those years ago. Only I wasn't some scared little faggot like Billy and this wasn't 1886. I wasn't going to hide myself. I wasn't going back in the closet to please my father or anyone else. Fuck it all! They couldn't change me and they won't hide me. I refused to be silenced.

"No," I replied, my voice steady and strong despite the way my body was shaking.

"What did you say?" Craig bristled, as if he couldn't believe that anyone would defy him.

"I said, 'No'. I'm not going to hide myself or pretend to be something I'm not just so you can pretend to have a 'normal' son. I won't do it," I maintained stubbornly.

Craig seemed honestly surprised by my rebelliousness and for half a second I thought maybe he'd back down. Then he seemed to find his resolve and snarled back at me. "Fine! If that's what you want, so be it. But that's it, Tristan. I've had it. You either leave off all this 'gay shit', and come home with me right now, or you never come home again!"

I paused and mulled over his ultimatum but still couldn't see any way I'd be able to live the pretence he expected of me. So my answer was clear. "Never again," I said, my voice a little shaky from the emotion of it all, but my resolve was as solid as ever. "Did you hear me? I said, NEVER AGAIN!" Craig looked shocked that I'd choose my morals over his money, but what had I expected? "Go! Get the fuck out of here! Go on, Craig!" I screamed at him, now in almost as big a rage as he'd been in earlier. "I'm never coming home again. Never fucking again!"

"Tristan, stop," Brandon cautioned, his arms cinching more tightly around my waist and his face coming down to nuzzle at my ear. "He's not worth it. Let's just get the fuck out of here and go home."

I nodded wordlessly. Brandon reached down, slid an arm under my knees, and hefted me back up into a cradle hold. Then, without another word, he turned back to the tunnel door, snatched up my phone from the ledge where it had still been broadcasting the facetime call to Brandon's computer, and carried me out of the whirling chaos of the tiny storage room. I could hear Ian calling my name but then someone closed the door behind us and it was silent and dark and we were all alone once more.

*****

I truthfully don't remember how we made it back to the Triangle Building. I vaguely remember holding up my phone in flashlight mode to light our way while Brandon mostly carried me over and around all the obstacles and corners until we made it safely back to his apartment. I felt disconnected from it all. I didn't completely come back to myself until I felt the water from Brandon's shower pelting down on my skin from above. And damn that felt good. Washing away all the dirt and blood and anger and fear. Even the slight sting from the shampoo when Brandon began to wash my hair felt good as I knew it meant he was cleaning away the stain of that horrible scene. I looked down and saw that the water pouring off me was tinged with red and, as much as I didn't want to, I tried to push Brandon away. There was blood - lots of it - and even as out of it as I was, I still knew to protect him from touching it more than he already had.

"I can do it," I protested, shoving at his hands as I pushed myself away from his supportive body, which I hadn't realized I'd needed until it was too late. My body swayed and I could feel my legs shaking beneath me.

"Stop it, Tristan." Brandon's voice was stern, yet strangely soothing, as he pulled me back into his arms. "Let me wash you, for fuck sake. You're covered in all kinds of disgusting blood and shit from the tunnel and who knows what else."

I tried to pull away again, but he held me tighter.

"But I'm bleeding. It's getting all over you," I said weakly.

"I know," Brandon sighed loudly. "Just let me do this, okay? The water from the shower is rinsing it all away. I'm fine."

I nodded, which only made me feel dizzier than before. So I scrunched my eyes shut and wrapped my arms tighter around his waist as he worked at cleaning me up. But it was his purring baritone words that seemed to hold me up more than anything else.

"I'm so fucking proud of you, Tristan. The way you handled your dad . . . The way you stood up for yourself like that. I'm really fucking proud."

That's when it hit me. What my father had said to me - the ultimatum he'd given me - and I couldn't stop the tears from falling. It was a weird feeling; I had stopped loving my father a while ago, but hearing him talking to me like I meant absolutely fucking nothing to him, it had hurt like hell. I hadn't been prepared for that. I felt like a wuss for crying. Logically, I knew I was better off without him, so why was it affecting me so much.

"Shhh, it's okay. You're okay, Tristan. He's not worth it."

"I . . . I know. I don't know why I'm crying about it."

"Because he's your dad and you still love him."

I shook my head as I sobbed. "No, I don't. I hate him. I fucking hate him so much . . ."

Brandon nuzzled my cheek as he rubbed soothing circles on my back. "No you don't. You think you hate him. But you don't."

"No," I could feel the hate boiling up inside of me again. "I really do hate him, Brandon. How can you even think that I don't? After what he just did? What he said?"

"You hate what he's become, and I get that. You SHOULD hate that man. He's a disgusting bigot and doesn't deserve your love. But . . ." He was silent for a moment as though he was thinking carefully about what he wanted to say. "He hasn't always been like that, right? I bet you have good memories of him from when you were a kid; that's the Tristan who's crying. The Tristan that looked up to the man who protected him from whatever shit you were scared of as a kid. That's the Tristan who's hurt. It's okay for THAT Tristan to cry over what he's lost."

Eggy's reasoning made sense. Until I was a teenager, Craig had been a great dad. My father would chase the monsters I had imagined out of my room when I was little and, when I was a bit older, I would go to work with him and sit in his office doing my homework. Those times together were something we both looked forward to. When I was younger, he was always boasting to his friends about how smart I was, how I was going to do great things with my life, and I guess any kid would love that sort of attention.

"Yeah, I guess." I sniffled loudly.

"It's like . . . With Donal . . . *sigh* . . . I hate that man with everything in me. I hate what he did to me. He was a piece of shit. He was a nasty bully who took advantage of a young kid when I had no one else . . . But he wasn't always like that. Not to that extent anyway . . . When I first came to live here, and my Aunt was still alive, he'd take me to the park to play soccer. He would stand there proudly and watch me as I had a kick around with some of the other boys . . . Unfortunately, those happy moments didn't last very long. Yet, by the time he died, I wanted nothing more than to celebrate. I was free from him. Free from his controlling bullshit. But as much as I wanted to be happy, part of me was still fucking sad that he died, you know? I didn't WANT to be sad for him. I hated him. But I guess seven year old Brandon popped into my brain and, for a while at least, made me forget all that messed up shit he put me through . . . So, what I'm trying to say, Tristan, is . . . It's okay to grieve what you had. It doesn't make the hate you feel for him now any less valid."

See, Brandon got me. He understood exactly how I was feeling at that moment. I didn't care I had lost Craig - we hadn't been close since I came out - but I couldn't forget all those wonderful memories I still had from when I was a kid.

"Thank you, Brandon." I shivered under the cooling shower water.

"Come on, let's get you out of here. You're as clean as I can get you. Which is saying a lot, you know, because NOBODY knows how to clean better than me," he joked and I smiled even though I didn't feel like laughing quite yet.

I followed him out of the shower, walking straight into his arms, where he wrapped me in his largest, fluffiest towel and pulled me into the bedroom.

"Lay down," he ordered, pointing to the bed.

I did as I was told and watched as he wrapped his own towel tighter around his waist. Then he walked towards me, pulled my towel off, and proceeded to crawl up the bed until he was kneeling above me, his own longer legs straddling my thighs. I felt small with him perched over me like that, but it was a comfortable smallness; like, I knew I'd be okay, because my smallness meant his largeness could contain me. For once it was okay for me to be small, and scared and in need of protection.

"Hi," I smiled up shyly into his dark hazel eyes.

He returned the smile.

"Other than your head, do you hurt anywhere else?" Brandon asked softly. "Do these hurt?" His fingers had found their way to my neck and were stroking softly at the obvious bruises that had been left there by Craig's fingers.

I nodded gently, not wanting him to stop what he was doing. "Yeah. A little."

As soon as I said that, he took his fingers away, and I heard myself moan in protest. But I needn't have worried because his lips soon replaced them. For about half a second I contemplated asking him, teasingly, if he was gonna kiss ALL my booboos better. Then I told myself not to be a complete moron, because of course I didn't want him to STOP kissing me - I never wanted him to stop kissing me - and I forced myself to just keep my fucking mouth shut. Which was a smart idea because, luckily, the kissing didn't stop at the bruises on my throat. Instead, my personal Florence Nightingale continued on, his lips leaving gentle caresses all down my neck, over my chest, along the line from my sternum to my navel, and beyond. I was a little disappointed when they took a detour just before they reached the good stuff, but the kisses trailing sideways over the thin skin covering my hip and then down one of my thighs almost made up for it, and I was in no real hurry.

But then everything went to hell again when the lips reached about calf level. "What the . . . ? Brandon's head popped up and he started to run his hands over my leg. "Oww!" He held up his finger so I could see the welling drop of blood at the tip.

"What the hell?"

I sat up so I could better see what was going on and noticed the smattering of small, angry wounds dotted all over my left ankle and calf. I hadn't noticed those injuries until just then; I'd been too focused on the more serious and painful wounds to my head and neck. Now that it had been brought to my attention, though, the previously dull throbbing in that area became much more insistent.

Brandon, who was hunched over so he could inspect the area more carefully, reached down and carefully plucked something out of one of those tiny gashes, holding whatever he'd found up to the light. "It looks like glass. How'd you get glass in your leg?"

I thought back to the altercation with Craig. It was all a little hazy - fear, adrenaline and getting your head bashed into the wall will do that to you - but I distinctly remembered when Craig had dropped his glass tumbler to the floor and it had shattered into a million pieces. I hadn't felt anything when it happened, probably because I was too busy trying to peel his fingers off from around my neck, but now it definitely hurt.

"Craig dropped his whiskey glass," I explained to Nurse Egbert, hissing loudly as he plucked another small piece of glass from my leg, this time with a pair of tweezers he kept in his bedside drawer - I wasn't entirely sure what he used them for, as my hairy lover was . . . you know . . . always incredibly hairy, but they did come in handy this once, so yay.

"Stay still," Brandon ordered brusquely before he proceeded to inspect and prod and tweez at my ankle for another ten painful minutes. "Shit, that's quite a bit of shrapnel in there, but I think I got it all. Fucking snobs and their expensive leaded crystal stemware; that shit will cut through clothing, not to mention skin, like it was butter. Hang on a sec longer and I'll bandage that for you."

Before I could protest or tell him that I didn't think the small cuts, despite their multiplicity, needed a full-on bandage, he was gone. A minute later he was back with the most extensive first-aid kit I'd ever seen. It was the size of a small piece of luggage. I mean, hell, this guy was ready for the apocalypse or something. I'm pretty sure most hospitals aren't that well-equipped. I didn't say anything, though, because I didn't want to interrupt my knight in shining armor as he ministered to me.

"There, I think that should take care of it," Brandon concluded as he applied the last piece of surgical tape and sat back to survey his work, nodding his head in approval.

"Thank you for taking such good care of me," I told him, smiling at him sincerely.

I watched as he shrugged his shoulders nonchalantly, never meeting my eye, and then began to put all his supplies back away in the first-aid kit.

"I mean it, Brandon. Thank you," I reached out with one hand to stop his fussing, hoping he'd look in my eyes and know how much I meant my gratitude.

Brandon cleared his throat nervously, stubbornly refusing to make any sort of eye contact at all. My man really didn't like it when I showered him with praise. He was so cute when he played bashful, although nowadays he didn't have that bushy beard to hide behind so I could see him even when he wanted to hide.

"Well, good . . . So, um . . . Now that you're all taken care of . . ." he said, stumbling slightly over his words. "How 'bout you take care of me?"

I looked up at him quickly, I wasn't sure what he was trying to say - and he wasn't making it easy as he was still refusing to look at me - but why would Brandon need taken care of? Had he been injured in the fight with my dad? I felt terrible that I'd been so worried about myself I hadn't even thought to ask if HE was okay. I can be such an ass sometimes.

"Of course, Brandon. I'm sorry about my father. I never meant for you to get in the middle of all that. I'll never forgive him for hurting you. Just let me check you over. Lay down," I smiled, moving out from the center of the mattress so there was room for him to lie down in my place.

"No, it's not that . . . I'm not hurt," Eggy cleared his throat nervously, making me so fucking confused.

"Okaay . . ."

I was thoroughly perplexed. If he wasn't hurt, why did he need me to take care of him? Then I watched as Brandon stood up, pulled his towel off, and exposed his beautiful body to me. His dick was right at eye level and I wanted nothing more than to take him into my mouth then and there. But before I could even touch him, he'd moved around me and flopped down on the bed, rolling over onto his front and burying his face in his folded arms with his bare ass on display, ever so slightly wiggling as though it was trying to get my attention.

By the time I managed to tear my eyes away from his glorious ass, I noticed he'd somehow managed to locate a condom and was now holding it out to me - his head still resting heavily on his arms so that he wasn't looking at me - waving that little foil packet in the air like a flag. Even then it took me a full sixty seconds before I figured out what he was asking for. When I did finally cotton on, holy fucking shit, I couldn't believe that was what he wanted.

Was he actually suggesting that he wanted me to fuck him? Was that really what he was asking me to do? I was in shock. Brandon giving up control like that hadn't even been on my radar. Especially not when we'd only just reached the fucking stage a few days before. But, even though I was surprised and a little unsure, I sure as hell wasn't gonna wait around and let a good thing like that pass me by.

I snatched the packet out of his hand and rolled it on as fast as I could without causing myself any serious damage. I grabbed the good lube off the nightstand and climbed onto the bed next to my man. Then I kinda froze because . . . Well, because this was big. This was really big. Huge even. And serious. I needed to do this right. For both of us.

I ran my left hand lightly down his back, outlining his spine with the tips of my fingers, and enjoying the way his muscles rippled under my touch. When I got to his glutes, I could feel him tensing up, so I stopped, letting my hand linger, just cupping the rounded edge of him with my palm until his cold skin warmed to match my own body temperature. When I felt him relaxing again, I let my hand drift over to his other buttock so my right hand could join in on the fun. At the same time I repositioned myself so I could settle on the bed between his thighs, using my knees to spread his legs wider until I had room to proceed. My kneading thumbs eventually drifted low enough to tease apart the softly fuzzed cheeks, revealing a perfectly star-shaped knot. Making use of the lube, I went to work, gently prying, intent on untying that protective knot. Working at it. Worrying it. Jimmying at the locked opening. Hell, by that point I wanted to get inside him so bad I didn't care what I had to do to accomplish the feat. If I had to fucking break in, so be it. Brandon didn't call me his Burglar for nothing. While all this was going through my mind, I was also thinking to myself how glad I was that nobody could hear my mental commentary on what I was doing, because that much purple prose was just pathetic. Whatever.

"Hey, Romeo? I think that's probably good enough," Brandon's sultry voice broke into my inner monologue - thank fuck - and reminded me to focus. "I know it's been awhile, but I'm not exactly a virgin, you know. I'm not gonna break or anything. So, if you wouldn't mind . . ."

"Right. Sorry. I got a little distracted," I muttered.

"I could tell," he smirked, and I don't know how I knew he was smirking, cuz I still couldn't see his face, but I just KNEW he was smirking at me, you know?

"Moving on," I declared.

After which, things seemed to flow more smoothly. I grabbed a pillow and shoved it under his hips, stretched myself out so I was in the right position, and used one hand to align myself, before slowly, carefully but confidently, pushing against the restricting twist of muscles. A heartbeat of resistance later and they finally gave enough to let me slide in.

There it was. I was doing it. I was inside my formerly-hairy hermit. I was fucking Brandon! Shit! I could hardly believe it was happening. I was seriously the luckiest SOB on the fucking planet because I was getting to fuck the most gorgeous man who'd ever lived! Look at me go! I felt like Superman or something. I was INVINCIBLE! Fuck my father! Fuck all homophobes ever! Fuck the world! Nothing else would ever matter now that I had this!

"You can go ahead and move now, Sunshine," Brandon's voice directed, breaking into my elation.

"Oh, yeah . . . Well, here goes nothing," I mumbled to myself as I started moving.

Once I really got going it was even better. I mean, I'm not one to brag, but - oh, who am I kidding, I love to brag - it was AMAZING. I may have had more experience at bottoming, but I was one fucking fantastic top, too. I had my usually reserved Stylite moaning and writhing and . . . Well, you get the idea. Plus, Brandon and I just meshed, you know? So, when he finally came and we both collapsed into a soggy, sweaty, sated heap, I don't think I'd ever felt more elated in my entire life.

So, yeah, that happened.

I'd also, for those few precious moments, forgotten completely about the Club, my father, my injuries, and even the fact that I was now a penniless, disinherited, soon-to-be-former art student, with no future prospects whatsoever. Which, now that I thought about it, had probably been Brandon's intent all along. At least, I HAD forgotten until the way we'd landed, laying on our sides with our legs tangled together, put too much pressure against my cut up ankle, and then it all came back to me in a rush. Welcome to my emotional roller coaster, folks. I went from the high of making love to my wonderful, caring boyfriend, to utter desolation in sixty seconds flat.

"Shhh. It's okay. You're gonna be fine," I heard Brandon crooning in my ear, not even realizing until he said something that I'd been sobbing. "We're both gonna be just fine. We'll fix this. We can do anything together, Brat. Right? Come on. I mean, hell, if you can fix me - get me to the point, after just a few weeks, where I not only left the building for the first time in a decade, but feel semi-sorta-not-totally freaked out sitting here in bed with cum smeared all over me - you can do anything, Tristan."

I snorted through my tears and just held onto him tighter. "I guess. I mean, I even got you to like snuggling."

"Yeah…No. This isn't snuggling. This is comforting a sad twink. I still don't snuggle."

"Riiiiiight," I kidded him.

Then I snuggled even closer to him and we fell asleep.

*****

Chapter 11

Happy Ending

I awoke, who knew how many hours later, being rolled to the side as the bed sheet covering the mattress was slowly tugged out from under me.

I blinked around me in the dimness, which was only barely alleviated by the light spilling out through the open bathroom door. There was a dark, hulking figure looming at the foot of the bed. It was that shadowy creature who was trying to take away the sheets while I was sleeping on them.

"Eggy? What are you doing?" I rasped, my voice thick with sleep.

"Nothing. Just go back to sleep," he replied as he continued pulling at the sheet.

"Egbert . . ."

He stopped pulling and sighed. "I couldn't sleep. The sheets are all dirty. I didn't have a condom on the last time and, well, I just can't sleep on them like that," he confessed. If I could actually see his face in the dark, I was sure I'd see him blushing, since I could hear it in his voice. "I was trying to do it without waking you up, though."

"Oh you silly, sweet, ridiculous man," I laughed, rolling out of the bed to help him change the sheets. "I don't mind you waking me up, you derp. Come on. I'll help you clean up and then it'll be done faster."

So we changed the sheets. We started a load of dirty laundry. I watched as Eggy disinfected the nightstands and the lube bottle and everything else that might have come into contact with any trace of cum. Then we both took a shower, because there was dried cum all over both of us as well. But then Eggy started to scrub at the counters in the bathroom too, and I had to put my foot down or we would have been up all night cleaning every surface in the damned six story tall building. I realized it was just Brandon's reaction to having given up control to me in that last round of love making - I mean, I totally get that, right - but I was too tired just then to deal with it. So, I forcibly took the bottle of spray cleaner out of his hands, put it away under the counter where it belonged, and led him back to the freshly made up bed. I could tell he was still too restless to sleep, though, so I went with a distraction kiss attack.

"There. Feel better?" I asked when we finally came up for air a few minutes later.

"Definitely," he chuckled and pulled me closer into the enveloping circle of his arms.

I relaxed and let my head fall onto his shoulder, fitting myself into the hollow there that seemed perfectly shaped to the size of my skull, and let my fingers play across the skin of his chest.

Damn, it felt good to be there. To just lie there together like that, quiet and peaceful and calm. After all the hullabaloo of the previous night, I needed that sense of serenity. Although, just acknowledging the fact that I needed some peace brought to mind my troubles again and kinda destroyed the moment.

Damn, my overactive mind. Sometimes I wish it came with an off switch.

"Brandon?"

"Hmmm?"

"I never thanked you for coming to get me and saving me from my dad," I ventured quietly. "That was pretty amazing, by the way."

I could feel the shoulder under my head shrugging. After a long pause, he added, "we were talking and then I saw him kick the door in and start screaming at you and I had the most vivid flashback to this one time when Donal did the same thing, you know? I had been hiding from him in my room - I don't even remember what it was I'd done wrong, but I knew he'd be coming after me - and he kicked the door in just like Craig did. Then Donal pulled me out of the room by my fucking hair. It hurt like hell. I think I had a bald spot there for about a month afterwards. Anyway, Donal was stinking drunk . . . Why is it that drunk men are always stronger than they would be sober?" I shrugged but didn't speak because I didn't want to interrupt his narrative. "Yeah, it was . . . It was bad."

"I'm sorry you had to live like that, Brandon."

He bent his neck so he could reach my temple with a kiss. "It was a long, long time ago, Sunshine." I squeezed his waist in reply, which seemed to be just the support he needed to continue. "But I just couldn't let the same thing happen to you. I couldn't . . . I didn't even really think about it. I just knew I had to come get you."

"Why'd you come through the tunnels, though?" I had been curious about that. "I thought you hated the very thought of them."

"I do. But I guess I hate the idea of going out into the street more," he explained. "I'd been up in my office while we were facetiming but the second your dad broke into the room and came after you, I took off, running down the stairs so fast it's a miracle I didn't trip and break my neck. But when I came to the lobby door, I just COULDN'T open it. I couldn't make my hand even touch the lock to turn it. I knew I didn't have time to waste, though, because every second I fucked around was another second your dad could hurt you. Which is when I thought about the tunnels. At the moment, that just seemed like the lesser of two evils. So I just did it."

"I'm thankful you did. If you hadn't arrived when you had, I don't know what would have happened. I was about to pass out. Meanwhile, that idiot Ian was just standing there watching as my father strangled me. Fucker."

"That little pissant was your fucking date?" Brandon scoffed. "He looked even more pathetic up close than he had that time I saw him through the window."

"Yeah, you're not wrong about the pathetic part."

"So, then, what's this your father said about you kissing him?" Brandon pried, a distinct edge of jealousy evident in his voice. "I didn't hear that wrong, did I? You actually kissed that curly haired greaseball?"

I huffed and shook my head. "It wasn't a 'kiss' kiss; it was just Ian being an ass. Besides, I didn't kiss him; he kissed me. Trust me, kissing Ian is the last thing I ever want to do again."

"Good. Because I don't want that flat-assed skank's lips anywhere near you ever again," Brandon declared rather more loudly than needed since my head was only about three inches from his mouth.

"Awww, Eggy, does that mean you intend to assert exclusive kissing rights to my lips?" I teased him.

"Actually . . . Yes. Yes, I do."

That got my attention. I sat up, turning so I could look at him, because I didn't want to misunderstand where this was going. I really had just been kidding about the exclusive lips thing. I mean, Eggy and I were just so NEW. I know I had been growing more and more serious about him the whole time - hell, I had even admitted to myself that I LOVED him, although I hadn't yet been brave enough to say it out loud - but I hadn't been sure Brandon was there yet. However, it seemed that he'd got there somehow too.

"Look, Tristan, I want to be up front here. I have no idea where this thing between us is going. I'm still pretty fucked up - I know that - and I plan to work on it. But whatever we do have, it . . . It's important . . . I don't want to fuck it up. I'll understand if you're not ready . . . It's just that I really can't stand the idea of you kissing that Ian guy . . . Or, any guy, really . . . And it's not just that I don't want their germs getting on your lips," he said, trying to lighten the mood, although I could tell there was still a little bit of serious concern hidden in there. "Let's face it, with me stuck inside here, and you out there, you have a lot more options than me. I'm okay with that. But even if you're out fucking every other guy you see, I would still like it if this," he leaned in and kissed me, gently, tenderly, with only a barely-there pressure, but so sweetly that I almost melted, "could be only for us."

Did I say I ALMOST melted? Strike that. I COMPLETELY melted. Seriously, could this guy get any more amazing? He just basically told me he loved me, in his typical understated Eggy way. Fuck, I simply adored my hermit. So of course I immediately agreed, because I'm not a fucking moron here. Assuming I even wanted to kiss anyone other than Eggy - which, for the record, I didn't - I'd happily give that up for the chance to cement things with Brandon. Because I really DID love this man. I loved everything about him. I especially loved the way he had been willing to fight even his most paralyzing fears to come save me from my father. So, fuck it all! He could have all my kisses forever. I didn't have even a shred of a doubt about that.

"It's a deal. From here on out, my lips belong only to you, Eggy. Now, come here, you big dork, and let me show you what I can do with them," I ordered and pulled him down so I could deliver my lips to him immediately.

*****

So, yeah, that all happened more than a year ago, just before my twentieth birthday, although it feels like forever. Since then, things have gotten better and better. My life now is pretty much totally perfect, actually. And I owe it all to my Hairy Hermit.

Craig - I refused to call him my father after what he did - predictably followed through with his threat to disinherit me. Big whoop. He even tried to drain the funds from my education trust, but was stopped when I went to court and got an injunction against him. Those funds were deposited in the trust by my grandparents, not him, and even if he had put the money in, he couldn't take it back out without incurring huge tax penalties, so when I threatened to report him to the IRS, he finally backed down. Which means I'm still okay on the money front for the time being and haven't had to drop out of school. It's hilarious though, because Craig really thought he was messing with some 'pathetic little fairy', but after I wiped the floor with him in court, he had no idea what hit him. Craig:0/Tristan:1.

I'm almost finished with my junior year at TAIP. It's going pretty well, to be honest. My grades are good and I've been recognized by several of my professors for my talent. My work has been included in several student showcases and I've even had a few feelers from local galleries about showing my work commercially. So, things are generally good on that front.

The big news, though, is that I have now officially moved into the Triangle Building with Egbert. It happened little by little, all last spring, with me gradually staying over more nights out of every week until about June, when Darla finally asked, if I wasn't going to use my room anymore, could she let a girlfriend she worked with move in. I was a little worried about bringing the topic up with Brandon, despite how well we were getting on, but he surprised me. He said he thought I already HAD moved in, seeing as all my clothing and art supplies had long since taken up residence in his guest room and my ass had formed a permanent dent in his mattress. After that I figured what the hell and just moved my few remaining personal possessions in for good.

How's that working, you ask? Actually, it's not bad. Brandon still has his fears and his rituals and some days are more difficult than others, but we deal with it. I've had to become much tidier than I ever was before; which isn't a bad thing, to be honest. Once the meds kicked in, though, things got a lot better pretty damn quickly. Within just a couple months, his more serious panic attacks had abated and we started working on the Cognitive Behavioral Therapy stuff more diligently. By summer I was able to tempt him outside the building. By fall I had him in therapy with a friend of Marcy's who specializes in OCD and Complex PTSD. I know that OCD isn't the kind of thing you ever just get over, but he's learning ways to cope with the stressors that make it worse. Basically, there are more good days than bad days now, so I can't complain.

Strangely, it seemed like the confrontation with Craig was the turning point for Brandon. Once he started therapy and became able to verbalize his feelings more easily, he explained that the experience had been remarkably freeing. He told me he was so proud of me for the way I'd stood up to my father; something he'd never been able to do where Donal was concerned. He was especially impressed with the fact I'd told Craig to fuck off; he said that had taken balls, and proven to him just how strong

I was, despite my twinkie physique. Watching me insist that I wouldn't take shit or let myself be browbeaten into submission, had inspired him to confront his own issues. Knowing he had braved those tunnels on his own and had mopped the floor with Craig's ass didn't hurt his self confidence either.

So I guess having to suffer through a third head injury in just over a month and becoming estranged from my father in the process was a good thing?

Anyway, we've come a long way since then. I have a gorgeous, intelligent, caring, boyfriend and we're living together in his architecturally amazing building. I've got my art. He's got his technical writing job, which I think is boring as shit, but which makes him pretty decent money without stressing him out from having to deal with people.

We've even got plans for the future; namely, Eggy is gonna slowly start renovating the building and leasing out the lower floors to actual tenants. I promised him I would handle pretty much ALL the interaction with both the construction crews and the new tenants. I haven't told him yet, but my long-term plan is to eventually remodel the entire building into a bed and breakfast-style hotel with a brewpub on the street level, conference/meeting rooms on the first floor and guest suites on the second through fifth floor. I've been working on the plans for how I want to decorate everything, including murals that I plan to paint throughout showing off the history of the building and the Golden Triangle area in general. It's gonna be great. I know Brandon will warm up to my ideas eventually. He's always been unable to resist my charms, despite all my crazy ideas, poor guy.

Oh, and did I mention the sex? There's LOTS of it. Soooo much sex. Brandon's totally loosened up in that regard. He says that the same sense of inner strength he found after the fight with Craig, the one that let him finally take control of his agoraphobia, has also freed him up in the sex department. Thank the gay gods and everything that is fucking holy! But it's true. He doesn't even make me wear an extra condom when he fucks me these days. Progress, right? Of course, he still prefers that we shower immediately afterwards - because, OCD still - but that's all good, because we usually get to have a second go round in the shower. So you're not going to hear ME complaining. Yeah, this bottom boy is happily fulfilled. And Brandon, whenever he gets the occasional itch, gets himself fulfilled too.

It's really all good. Okay, more than good. It's fucking fabulous! Not that I'm bragging or anything.

Today, however, is the biggest test yet of all those good things that have happened to us over the past year. Today, I'm taking Eggy to meet the gang at the Diner. Did I say big? I meant huge. Can you just imagine all the mental preparation this took; he's going out in public, having to meet a whole gaggle of new people who will probably want to touch him in some way - if I know Sharon, she'll want to not only give him a bear hug, but probably kiss his cheek as well - and if that wasn't enough, I'm going to try and get him to order something. Hell, it took me almost an hour just to get him out of the building, and I had to promise to pack the half dozen travel-packs of wet wipes he insisted we bring along 'just in case'. But here we are, standing outside the Diner. Now, if I can just get him through the front door.

"You ready for this, Eggy?" I asked, his sweaty palm clenched tightly against my own.

I could tell from the rapid pace of his breathing and the way he was biting at his bottom lip that he was pretty agitated, but he had told me before that he really wanted this, so I was going to do whatever I could to make it happen.

"I don't know . . ." he muttered.

"You've got this, Brandon. We've been planning this little lunch adventure for weeks. Your therapist thinks you're ready for it.

I think you're ready for it. Even you said you were ready for it just yesterday. And you know it's not going to be as difficult as you're making it out to be in your head, right?" I reassured him, taking one more step closer to the entrance and pulling him along in my wake. "Besides, I'm going to be right there with you, so it'll all be fine."

He looked at me with so much trust just then that I thought I might fall in love with him all over again. "Okay. Just . . . Don't let go," he ordered, giving my hand another squeeze.

"I promise. I will never let go, Jack. I'll never let go."

Brandon shook his head and laughed as he looked at me; the mood lightened just a little with my teasing. Brandon swore he hated 'Titanic', but still always found the time to sit down and watch it with me, which was sadly more often than I would like to admit. He always gave me shit when I quoted lines from the movie to him, though.

"You have watched that fucking movie enough to know that Rose lets go . . . It doesn't matter how many times you watch it, the ending won't change, as much as I know you would like it to."

"Okay, alright. I get it." I laughed along with him now. I love it when he teases me like this.

"But I mean it, Tristan . . . Don't let go."

"I promise. I'm not letting go. I already told you that. And you know I'm tenacious as hell, so you can count on me."

He nodded, straightening up his shoulders and standing as tall as he could, and then giving me a crooked little smile. Did I mention how much I adore that crooked little smile of his? If I hadn't been on a mission just then, I would have gladly taken him aside and kissed the fuck out of him for that damned adorable smile. Just don't tell HIM I was using the word 'adorable' in reference to him - even in my head - because that would be a whole 'nother battle, and we didn't have time for that.

"Good. Now, let's get this bread!" I voiced my battle cry as I pulled open the door and led my man inside to the tinkle of the bell over the entrance.

"Tristan! There you are, Sweetie!" Shar roared in greeting the second the door closed behind us. I could feel Brandon tensing up and taking a step back as the red-wigged-wonder came bar-relling towards us, her voice seemingly louder than ever. "And you finally brought your mysterious boyfriend too! Come here and let me get a good look at you, Stud."

"Yes, Shar. This is HIM," I started with the introductions. "Bran-don Kinney, meet Sharon Northrup. Shar is the manager of the Diner, my boss, and the self-appointed surrogate mother of all gay boys in the Pittsburgh Metropolitan Area." Eggy already knew all that, of course, because I talked about these folks pretty much constantly, but I thought it was only polite to give Shar her official due.

I could tell Sharon was just dying to sweep in, the way she usually did, and give both of us the full Northrup treatment, complete with rib-crushing bear hugs, smeared-lipstick kisses, and maybe even a pinch to a buttcheek here and there, but thankfully she restrained herself. I had warned her in advance - I'd warned EVERYBODY in advance - that Brandon did not like to be touched by strangers, and threatened to break the fingers of anyone who tried it. Apparently, I'm scarier than I look, because even Sharon remembered and controlled herself.

"Well, now. Aren't you just the hottest thing this place has seen since the chili Raul concocted for the Pink Plate Special last week," Shar summed up her appraisal of my boyfriend. "I can see why Tristan's fallen, hook, line and sinker for a beauty like you, Brandon!"

"Enh. I don't know what you're talking about, Shar. I'm only with him cuz he provides artistically-pleasing living accomodations." Brandon squeezed my hand and out of the corner of my eye I could see a small smile on his face, although I knew he'd probably make me pay for my bratiness later. "I AM an artist, after all. If anyone deserves to live in an architectural showplace like the Triangle Building, it's me."

"It's nice to meet you, Sharon. Tristan has told me all about you," Brandon interrupted, trying to be the responsible one, as always.

"All true, I'm sure." Shar laughed loudly then pointed us towards the big booth in the back corner. "Well, take a seat with the rest of the boys. They don't bite . . . unless you ask them to, that is."

We didn't even make it all the way there, though, before the rest of my friends were on their feet to welcome us. They all had these stupidly big grins on their faces and it seemed like they were on their best behavior - as I'd ordered - all except for Spencer. As soon as Spencer saw Brandon his mouth fell open and he started fanning himself with his napkin.

"Well, now, Baby! Don't I just wanna spread you on a cracker and eat you for lunch," Spence gushed.

I could feel myself rolling my eyes at my eccentric friend's words. I knew Spencer would be instantly attracted to my man. Who wouldn't? And that's okay; he can look as long as he doesn't touch.

"Guys, this is Brandon. Brandon, this is Mitch, Edward, and Spencer," I explained, pointing to each one as I said their name. "Mitch is Sharon's son."

"I thought you ALL were," Brandon teased. I could tell he was slightly nervous, but I was already so proud of him. He was cracking jokes and being his delightfully delicious self.

"That's true," Mitch laughed. "But I'm . . ."

"He's the only one I pushed out through my vagina," Sharon interjected, cracking up at her own joke and throwing a bunch of menus down onto the table. "Call me over when you boys are ready to order."

Mitch moved over to join Edward and Spencer on the far side of the booth, giving me and Brandon room to slide in on the near side. I noticed, out of the corner of my eye, the way Brandon very carefully did not touch anything, but I wasn't going to give him a hard time about it seeing as he was actually doing really well. So far so good, right?

"Shar is EXACTLY the way you described her," Brandon commented with an amused smile aimed at the waitress' back as she bustled around behind the counter and yelled obscenities at both the cook and the customers.

"And you're exactly the way Tristan described you too," Edward piped up, looking appreciatively at Brandon from where he'd been shoved into the corner of the booth. "Here we all thought you were just making up this imaginary wonder of boyfriendly virtues."

"Sorry to disappoint, Eddy, but it's all true. He really is as gorgeous and smart as I told you," I bragged, rightfully so. "Not to mention just as good in bed."

"Ahem, Brat . . ." Brandon elbowed me in the side, trying to shut me up, but no way was I gonna take back something that was true, even if I was embarrassing him. "So, you promised to buy me lunch, remember? Which is only fair after I've been supplying your bounteous bubble butt for all these months. It's about time you started to pay me back a little."

"As if you didn't adore my bubble butt just the way it is," I rejoined, picking up two of the menus waiting on the table and sliding one over till it was waiting on the table right in front of him.

As he looked down at the menu, I could feel Brandon's leg nervously bouncing up and down next to mine. I glanced over quickly and knew immediately what had set him off. I could just tell by looking at the laminated menu lying there that it was sticky and all kinds of gross. I didn't want to embarrass him by handing him an antibacterial wipe in front of everyone, so instead I took charge, reaching into my bag where I'd stashed all his wipes and pulling out a whole packet. Then I grabbed his menu away from him and started cleaning it.

"Sorry about the menus being all disgusting, Brandon. The breakfast crowd is known to get the syrup from their waffles practically everywhere. Usually, when I'm working, I wipe them all down before I hand them out to customers, but sometimes a few get missed."

I efficiently cleaned off his menu, back and front, and then folded the wet wipe in half and used it to give the table a quick swab too. I didn't care what the guys thought about ME being finicky or cleaning the table; if they gave me shit about it later, I'd just say something about not wanting my boyfriend to see what a greasy dump it was the first time he ate there. Besides, it really was a little gross having the menus covered with grime like that all the time. Now that I'd noticed it, I'd be cleaning them off more diligently in the future.

After I stashed the dirty wipe in the pocket of my bag, I reached under the table and put my hand on Brandon's still-bouncing knee, feeling him calm down almost immediately, and knew we'd weathered that small crisis. No problemo! See, we could so do this going out to have lunch and meeting people thing. Piece of cake.

By the time we'd got the menus sorted out, Shar was back to take our order. She plunked down waters for everyone, pulled several pre-wrapped cutlery sets out of the pocket of her apron, licked the pencil she pulled out from behind her ear, and then started asking everyone what they wanted. I could tell Brandon was inwardly cringing at pretty much everything he saw, and just dying to clean it all before it came into contact with his skin, but doing his best to resist the obsession at the same time. I was so fucking proud of him right then I could have crowed. My Stylite was being such a trooper. Nevertheless I grabbed his hand under the table and held on tight, just to let him know I had his back if he needed me. Our fingers interlocked tightly, as though he could feel my confidence radiating through, from my hand to his.

Before our food came, the doorbell rang out again, and the next thing I knew, there were three more familiar faces hovering around our booth.

"Hey, Brandon," Molly crooned, batting her eyes at my lover in her most coquettish, teenaged way.

Mom and Molly had, of course, met Brandon a long time before this. Mom wasn't about to let me move in with someone she'd never even met, so Brandon had bravely invited them over for dinner early on. He did remarkably okay with them around, even. I'd told Mom about the OCD thing right from the beginning, but she was okay with it. She said she'd rather have me living with a neat freak than a total slob, and I had to agree with her on that one. So, except for my idiot sister's stupid crush on my boyfriend, it was all good.

"Miss Molly. You're looking lovelier than ever today," Brandon flirted right back with her, prompting me to punch his thigh under the cover of the table, because I'd warned him not to encourage her - she was fifteen years old and completely smitten with him - I mean, who can blame her, but it was a tad bit annoying.

"Hello, Honey," Mom interrupted the flirt-fest with an apologetic shake of her head and a side eye for her incorrigible daughter. "Brandon. I hope you don't mind; I ran into Darla at the Heinz History Center this morning and she said she was meeting you two here for lunch, so I thought we might join you. If we're not imposing too much."

"Of course not. You're always welcome, Jennifer." Did I mention that Brandon had won Mom over pretty much from the get go with his elegant manners and oozing charm? Yeah, he had all the members of the Taylor family enthralled. Well, the members that count, that is.

"Yeah, I stopped into the museum to check out the newest installation - featuring a piece by none other than my best friend in the whole wide world - and found your mom there doing the same thing," Darla explained as she climbed into the empty booth behind us and then draped herself over the intervening seat back so she could glom all over me and kiss my cheek with a loud smacking noise. "I know I already saw the painting way back when you first did it, but I gotta say it looks even better now that it's in a fancy pants museum."

Oh, yeah. I forgot to add that the piece I'd done for my Art and Architecture class all those months ago - the one that had started it all - was currently being exhibited by the Heinz Museum in a show they were doing on the history of the Golden Triangle. Can you believe it? Yeah, seems like Mayor Peduto had been a guest at the TAIP Spring Student Art Show and had seen the work I'd created with all the historical references to the Triangle Building incorporated into the multimedia piece and had loved it. So, thanks to the Mayor's intervention, I'd been given a spot in the new Heinz exhibit. Quite the coup for an aspiring artist, wouldn't you say?

"It truly is a lovely piece, Tristan. The way you incorporated all those photos and found art objects and quotes into the painting, was inspired," my mother commented boastfully. "And the write up the curators did connecting the picture to the Journal you found, really brought the exhibit to life."

I had Brandon to thank for that little twist. After my piece had been accepted by the museum, it was Brandon who'd thought about including the Journal and told the curator about the secret love story that had inspired my creation. So now all of Pittsburgh knew about the gay love triangle that had almost brought down two of the City's most prominent families.

It's kinda fitting, don't you think, seeing as it was Billy's story that tied everything together.

As I looked around me at the circle of family and friends who had come together this afternoon to welcome a new member into their tribe, I admit I might have got a little misty. Because, just look at all the support and love Brandon and I had. All these people accepted us for who we were. We weren't being vilified for loving the wrong person or the wrong gender. We were celebrated for it.

No, not everyone was as accepting as this bunch. There were still bad people in the world. There were still bigots and homophobes, like my father, who would never understand. But little by little, in increments almost too small to measure, the world HAD changed for the better since Billy's time. Thankfully, Brandon and I were lucky enough to live in an era where we didn't have to sneak around, building underground tunnels and hiding ourselves away. We were lucky enough to be afforded the luxury of loving each other openly, without fear of recrimination or punishment.

Was it any wonder that, as I sat there contemplating the bounty of support around me, I felt a little guilty? Brandon and I had so much. And we owed all of it to the shadowy historical figures who had brought us together: Peebles, with his inspired architecture and resourcefulness; Billy, the gay youngling just trying to find his place in a world that ended up ostracizing him for his sexuality; and Jay, the epitome of the closeted gay man who was trapped by convention. Three men who'd never had a chance to live their reality the way Brandon and I were, solely because being gay in 1885 was unacceptable. The difference between the endings of my story, and that of poor Billy Carnegie, really made you think, you know?

Of course there was one thing that hadn't changed; the brick bastion known as the Triangle Building was still standing proudly, gracing Liberty Avenue with its elegant presence, more than a hundred years later. It was still drawing in overly-romantic gay boys eager to unearth its mysterious attractions. First Billy, now me. Somehow we'd both found love in those walls. So maybe I was wrong. Maybe the world hadn't really changed all that much after all?

"Hey, you," Eggy leaned over to whisper in my ear. "Did I lose you? Come on, Brat, you can't zone out and just leave me hanging with all your crazy friends. You're the one who wants us to all live together, Kumbaya, happily-ever-after, and all that shit. If you want your happy ending, you gotta help me out here."

When Brandon punctuated his demand with a completely spontaneous kiss to my cheek, I knew it was true. I'd found my happy ending. All thanks to that mysterious, triangular-shaped building, and the Sexy Stylite inside, who I just couldn't stay away from.

*****

About The Author

Tag Gregory

TAG is the author of the exciting time-travel romance novel, Time Blitz, as well as the brand new series, The Stylite Chronicles. TAG has been writing for almost a decade, starting out with a hesitant toe in the realm of fanfiction before venturing into the scarier world of self-publishing original works. With an eclectic background as a lawyer, microbiologist, all-around nerd, and adventurer, it's a wonder they even have time for writing, to be honest. TAG brings that off-kilter sense of humor, unbounded curiosity, a love of details, and astonishing powers of research to all their writing. If you are looking for a gripping story, with compelling characters that deal with real world issues, then you're in the right place.

About The Author

Lily Marie

Lily is the co-author of the thrilling time-travel romance, Time Blitz, and the brand new series, The Stylite Chronicles. Lily has been writing for several years, starting out with Tag in the world of fanfiction and eventually branching out into original fiction. Lily and Tag teamed up to write Time Blitz when Lily got the idea off an old BBC series and they decided to create their own WWII world. Lily is a native of the UK and also the more artistic of this writing duo.

<h1 style="text-align:center;">Books By This Author</h1>

Time Blitz

A time-travel, gay romance set in WWII London at the height of the Blitz

Stylite: Mystery

Book One in The Stylite Chronicles

Stylite: History

Book Two in The Stylite Chronicles

Stylite: Romance

Book Three in The Stylite Chronicles

Authors' Note

Thank you for reading! We hope you are enjoying our stories - our readers are what make this fun hobby into something so much more satisfying. If you want to get updates on when future books will be coming out or follow other happenings with the authors, you can follow us on Goodreads (Tag: TagWrites, Lily: LilyMarieAuthor), check out our Author pages on Amazon, or follow us on Twitter (Lily: @LilyMarieBooks). Enjoy!